THE
Postutopian
ADVENTURES OF
Darger
and
Surplus

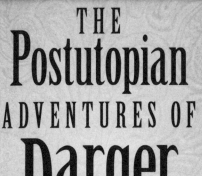

MICHAEL
SWANWICK

Subterranean Press 2020

First Edition

ISBN
978-1-59606-936-7

Subterranean Press
PO Box 190106
Burton, MI 48519

subterraneanpress.com

Manufactured in the United States of America

to my son
SEAN SWANWICK
for good and sufficient reasons

THE
Postutopian
ADVENTURES OF
Darger
and
Surplus

Table of Contents

• • • • • • • • • • • • • • • • •

INTRODUCTION
Mother Goose's
Errant Sons

Darger and Surplus are self-made men, not only in their choice of occupation but in how they came to appear on the page. I had been reading Thomas Pynchon's *Mason & Dixon* and, coming upon his quite marvelous talking dog, was seized by the desire to write a talking dog of my own. To avoid him being too like Pynchon's Learnèd Dog, I made my character anthropomorphic and a bit of a dandy. Because he had to be some-place, I set him down on the docks of a future London. Because he needed someone to talk with, I introduced Aubrey Darger, a man so nondescript in appearance that he could disappear in the smallest of crowds. Because they needed something to talk *about,* Darger invited Surplus to a public house, where he revealed that he was a confidence artist.

At which point, the two scoundrels ran away with the plot, leaving me hurrying after them, pen and paper in hand, crying, "Sirs! Sirs! Wait for me!"

I played catch-up through the story, always one step behind and considerably in the dark about what was coming next. It was only when I reached the last page of "The Dog Said Bow-Wow" that the pair, by now fast friends, revealed that there would be more stories to come.

I had never written a story series before, in large part because it is a rare character who, coming to the end of something I've written, would be eager for another go-round. Darger and Surplus, however, were different. They honestly believed that they were good people who were having a splendid time. On both counts they were completely delusional, of course. But their armor-clad egos, their unquenchable optimism, and their eternal conviction that the Big Score, the one that will make them rich for the rest of their lives, is only a scam away, made them perfect series characters.

Also, I found their company pleasant.

In real life, confidence artists are not at all likeable. They smile too much and they're far too eager to involve you in illegal acts. I've known my share of them, including a pair of Old School grifters who tried to take me with an updated version of the pigeon drop involving an ATM. In our fantasies, scam artists prey only upon the wicked. Not so in actuality. The Yellow Kid, probably the most likeable and certainly the most famous of a sketchy lot, often said, "You can't cheat an honest man." He may even have coined the saying. But he also claimed never to have met a man he couldn't cheat. So now you know what he would think of you, me, and the Dalai Lama.

But in our imaginings, confidence tricksters are criminal royalty, outranking even highwaymen and jewel thieves. They are who you and I would be if only we weren't so damnably honest. Living by our wits. Almost never resorting to violence. Traveling the world and leaving behind a trail of sexual conquests. Always staying in the finest hotels and never once pausing to consider the morality of our actions.

A word about the world my heroes inhabit…

I once asked Fritz Leiber if it was not possible that Newhon, the world inhabited by *his* adventurers, was actually a horror venue, disguised by the fact that Fafhrd and Mouser, those most urbane of swordsmen, always escaped the consequences of their actions at the end of each story. To this he responded, "Everything I have ever written is horror."

Something similar applies to the Postupian Era of Darger and Surplus. An unknown number of years before their adventures began, mankind's artificial creations rose up in rebellion. Humanity won the war that ensued—just barely. But in the process they lost almost all electronic and mechanical technology, though retaining the biological sciences. But while the demons and mad gods of the Internet were banished, they were not destroyed. In the lightless oceans of the worldwide electronic infrastructure they lurk, hate, and plot. At any given moment, implacable evil might erupt from underfoot to engulf an unsuspecting world in violence and horror.

Which is to say that Darger and Surplus' world is very much like our own. To lighten its underlying darkness, I gave the stories titles taken from Mother Goose.

After the unfortunate events of their first adventure, the two tricksters *extraordinaire* bounced around Europe, seemingly at random. At the end of each story they had a definite destination in mind; at the beginning of the next they had wound up somewhere else. The pair were endlessly distractible. Their ultimate destination, however, was always Moscow and so, when they finally reached it, I dedicated an entire novel, *Dancing with Bears,* to what happened to them there.

By then it was clear that, despite all their digressions, Darger and Surplus were on a purposive journey. What looked at first like Brownian motion was actually a trek eastward. By the time they reached Moscow, I had realized that they were on an accidental trip around the world. Inevitably, the second novel, *Chasing the*

Phoenix, was set in China. If ever there is a third novel, I suspect it will take place in San Francisco, that louche, near-lawless gateway to the Ancient New World. From there, it is obvious that Sir Blackthorpe Ravenscairn de Plus Precieux must return home to the Demesne of Western Vermont to confront certain secrets from his earlier life and come to terms with them, his name most definitely included. After which, London, where…

But let us pause here for a moment to look again at the significance of the journey Darger and Surplus are by now midway through. Let us ask ourselves what Fate has in mind for them that It would take such care with their itinerary.

Darger and Surplus are, unbeknownst to themselves, agents of chaos and change. Wherever they go, without intending it, they unearth dangerous revenants of the past. These, by preference, they leave for others to deal with, though when they must, they do their duty. And in their wake, the world is a different place.

By the time they return at last to London, where certain secrets from Darger's past await, they will find the city utterly changed and, with it, the world. In all innocence, they have been putting an end to the old age and ushering in a new one. No one, not even they themselves, will ever know how key a part they played in this.

Except the reader.

The stories collected here, along with novels *Dancing With Bears* and *Chasing the Phoenix,* are all that have been written to date. There will, I am certain, be more. How much or how many more I cannot say for I do not know.

Darger and Surplus, as usual holding their cards close to their vests, have not shared that information with me yet.

Michael Swanwick

The Dog Said
Bow-Wow

· · · · · · · · · · · · · · ·

The dog looked like he had just stepped out of a children's book. There must have been a hundred physical adaptations required to allow him to walk upright. The pelvis, of course, had been entirely reshaped. The feet alone would have needed dozens of changes. He had knees, and knees were tricky.

To say nothing of the neurological enhancements.

But what Darger found himself most fascinated by was the creature's costume. His suit fit him perfectly, with a slit in the back for the tail, and—again—a hundred invisible adaptations that caused it to hang on his body in a way that looked perfectly natural.

"You must have an extraordinary tailor," Darger said.

The dog shifted his cane from one paw to the other, so they could shake, and in the least affected manner imaginable replied, "That is a common observation, sir."

"You're from the States?" It was a safe assumption, given where they stood—on the docks—and that the schooner *Yankee Dreamer* had sailed up the Thames with the morning tide. Darger had seen its bubble sails over the rooftops, like so many rainbows. "Have you found lodgings yet?"

"Indeed I am, and no I have not. If you could recommend a tavern of the cleaner sort?"

"No need for that. I would be only too happy to put you up for a few days in my own rooms." And, lowering his voice, Darger said, "I have a business proposition to put to you."

"Then lead on, sir, and I shall follow you with a right good will."

⟡

THE DOG'S NAME was Sir Blackthorpe Ravenscairn de Plus Precieux, but "Call me Sir Plus," he said with a self-denigrating smile, and "Surplus" he was ever after.

Surplus was, as Darger had at first glance suspected and by conversation confirmed, a bit of a rogue—something more than mischievous and less than a cut-throat. A dog, in fine, after Darger's own heart.

Over drinks in a public house, Darger displayed his box and explained his intentions for it. Surplus warily touched the intricately carved teak housing, and then drew away from it. "You outline an intriguing scheme, Master Darger—"

"Please. Call me Aubrey."

"Aubrey, then. Yet here we have a delicate point. How shall we divide up the…ah, spoils of this enterprise? I hesitate to mention this, but many a promising partnership has foundered on precisely such shoals."

Darger unscrewed the salt cellar and poured its contents onto the table. With his dagger, he drew a fine line down the middle of the heap. "I divide—you choose. Or the other way around, if you please. From self-interest, you'll not find a grain's difference between the two."

"Excellent!" cried Surplus and, dropping a pinch of salt in his beer, drank to the bargain.

⟡

IT WAS RAINING when they left for Buckingham Labyrinth. Darger stared out the carriage window at the drear streets and worn buildings gliding by and sighed. "Poor, weary old London! History is a grinding-wheel that has been applied too many a time to thy face."

"It is also," Surplus reminded him, "to be the making of our fortunes. Raise your eyes to the Labyrinth, sir, with its soaring towers and bright surfaces rising above these shops and flats like a crystal mountain rearing up out of a ramshackle wooden sea, and be comforted."

"That is fine advice," Darger agreed. "But it cannot comfort a lover of cities, nor one of a melancholic turn of mind."

"Pah!" cried Surplus, and said no more until they arrived at their destination.

At the portal into Buckingham, the sergeant-interface strode forward as they stepped down from the carriage. He blinked at the sight of Surplus, but said only, "Papers?"

Surplus presented the man with his passport and the credentials Darger had spent the morning forging, then added with a negligent wave of his paw, "And this is my autistic."

The sergeant-interface glanced once at Darger, and forgot about him completely. Darger had the gift, priceless to one in his profession, of a face so nondescript that once someone looked away, it disappeared from that person's consciousness forever. "This way, sir. The officer of protocol will want to examine these himself."

A dwarf savant was produced to lead them through the outer circle of the Labyrinth. They passed by ladies in bioluminescent gowns and gentlemen with boots and gloves cut from leathers cloned from their own skin. Both women and men were extravagantly bejeweled—for the ostentatious display of wealth was yet again in fashion—and the halls were lushly clad and pillared in marble, porphyry and jasper. Yet Darger could not help noticing how worn the carpets were, how chipped and sooted the oil lamps. His sharp eye espied the remains of an antique electrical system, and traces as well of telephone lines and fiber optic cables from an age when those technologies were yet workable.

These last he viewed with particular pleasure.

The dwarf savant stopped before a heavy black door carved over with gilt griffins, locomotives, and fleurs-de-lis. "This is a door," he said. "The wood is ebony. Its binomial is Diospyros ebenum. It was harvested in Serendip. The gilding is of gold. Gold has an atomic weight of 197.2."

He knocked on the door and opened it.

The officer of protocol was a dark-browed man of imposing mass. He did not stand for them. "I am Lord Coherence-Hamilton, and this—" he indicated the slender, clear-eyed woman who stood beside him—"is my sister, Pamela."

Surplus bowed deeply to the Lady, who dimpled and dipped a slight curtsey in return.

The protocol officer quickly scanned the credentials. "Explain these fraudulent papers, sirrah. The Demesne of Western Vermont! Damn me if I have ever heard of such a place."

"Then you have missed much," Surplus said haughtily. "It is true we are a young nation, created only seventy-five years ago during the Partition of New England. But there is much of note to commend our fair land. The glorious beauty of Lake Champlain. The gene-mills of Winooski, that ancient seat of learning the Universitas Viridis Montis of Burlington, the Technarchaeological Institute of—" He stopped. "We have much to be proud of, sir, and nothing of which to be ashamed."

The bearlike official glared suspiciously at him, then said, "What brings you to London? Why do you desire an audience with the queen?"

"My mission and destination lie in Russia. However, England being on my itinerary and I a diplomat, I was charged to extend the compliments of my nation to your monarch." Surplus did not quite shrug. "There is no more to it than that. In three days I shall be in France, and you will have forgotten about me completely."

Scornfully, the officer tossed the credentials to the savant, who glanced at and politely returned them to Surplus. The small fellow sat down at a little desk scaled to his own size and swiftly made out a copy. "Your papers will be taken to Whitechapel and examined there. If everything goes well—which I doubt—and there's an opening—not likely—you'll be presented to the queen sometime between a week and ten days hence."

"Ten days! Sir, I am on a very strict schedule!"

"Then you wish to withdraw your petition?"

Surplus hesitated. "I... I shall have to think on't, sir."

Lady Pamela watched coolly as the dwarf savant led them away.

THE ROOM THEY were shown to had massively framed mirrors and oil paintings dark with age upon the walls, and a generous log fire in the hearth. When their small guide had gone, Darger carefully locked and bolted the door. Then he tossed the box onto the bed, and bounced down alongside it. Lying flat on his back, staring up at the ceiling, he said, "The Lady Pamela is a strikingly beautiful woman. I'll be damned if she's not."

Ignoring him, Surplus locked paws behind his back, and proceeded to pace up and down the room. He was full of nervous energy. At last, he expostulated, "This is a deep game you have gotten me into, Darger! Lord Coherence-Hamilton suspects us of all manner of blackguardry."

"Well, and what of that?"

"I repeat myself: We have not even begun our play yet, and he suspects us already! I trust neither him nor his genetically remade dwarf."

"You are in no position to be displaying such vulgar prejudice."

"I am not bigoted about the creature, Darger, I fear him! Once let suspicion of us into that macroencephalic head of his, and he will worry at it until he has found out our every secret."

"Get a grip on yourself, Surplus! Be a man! We are in this too deep already to back out. Questions would be asked, and investigations made."

"I am anything but a man, thank God," Surplus replied. "Still, you are right. In for a penny, in for a pound. For now, I might as well sleep. Get off the bed. You can have the hearth-rug."

"I! The rug!"

"I am groggy of mornings. Were someone to knock, and I to unthinkingly open the door, it would hardly do to have you found sharing a bed with your master."

❧❦❧

THE NEXT DAY, Surplus returned to the Office of Protocol to declare that he was authorized to wait as long as two weeks for an audience with the queen, though not a day more.

"You have received new orders from your government?" Lord Coherence-Hamilton asked suspiciously. "I hardly see how."

"I have searched my conscience, and reflected on certain subtleties of phrasing in my original instructions," Surplus said. "That is all."

He emerged from the office to discover Lady Pamela waiting outside. When she offered to show him the Labyrinth, he agreed happily to her plan. Followed by Darger, they strolled inward, first to witness the changing of the guard in the forecourt vestibule, before the great pillared wall that was the front of Buckingham Palace before it was swallowed up in the expansion of architecture during the mad, glorious years of Utopia. Following which, they proceeded toward the viewer's gallery above the chamber of state.

"I see from your repeated glances that you are interested in my diamonds, 'Sieur Plus Precieux,'" Lady Pamela said. "Well might you be. They are a family treasure, centuries old and manufactured to order, each stone flawless and perfectly matched. The indentures of a hundred autistics would not buy the like."

Surplus smiled down again at the necklace, draped about her lovely throat and above her perfect breasts. "I assure you, madame, it was not your necklace that held me so enthralled."

She colored delicately, pleased. Lightly, she said, "And that box your man carries with him wherever you go? What is in it?"

"That? A trifle. A gift for the Duke of Muscovy, who is the ultimate object of my journey," Surplus said. "I assure you, it is of no interest whatsoever."

"You were talking to someone last night," Lady Pamela said. "In your room."

"You were listening at my door? I am astonished and flattered."

She blushed. "No, no, my brother…it is his job, you see, surveillance."

"Possibly I was talking in my sleep. I have been told I do that occasionally."

"In accents? My brother said he heard two voices."

Surplus looked away. "In that, he was mistaken."

England's queen was a sight to rival any in that ancient land. She was as large as the lorry of ancient legend, and surrounded by attendants who hurried back and forth, fetching food and advice and carrying away dirty plates and signed legislation. From the gallery, she reminded Darger of a queen bee, but unlike the bee, this queen did not copulate, but remained proudly virgin.

Her name was Gloriana the First, and she was a hundred years old and still growing.

Lord Campbell-Supercollider, a friend of Lady Pamela's met by chance, who had insisted on accompanying them to the gallery, leaned close to Surplus and murmured, "You are impressed, of course, by our queen's magnificence." The warning in his voice was impossible to miss. "Foreigners invariably are."

"I am dazzled," Surplus said.

"Well might you be. For scattered through her majesty's great body are thirty-six brains, connected with thick ropes of ganglia in a hypercube configuration. Her processing capacity is the equal of many of the great computers from Utopian times."

Lady Pamela stifled a yawn. "Darling Rory," she said, touching the Lord Campbell-Supercollider's sleeve. "Duty calls me. Would you be so kind as to show my American friend the way back to the outer circle?"

"Or course, my dear." He and Surplus stood (Darger was, of course, already standing) and paid their compliments. Then, when Lady Pamela was gone and Surplus started to turn toward the exit, "Not that way. Those stairs are for commoners. You and I may leave by the gentlemen's staircase."

The narrow stairs twisted downward beneath clouds of gilt cherubs-and-airships, and debouched into a marble-floored hallway. Surplus and Darger stepped out of the stairway and found their arms abruptly seized by baboons.

There were five baboons all told, with red uniforms and matching choke collars with leashes that gathered in the hand of an ornately mustached officer whose gold piping identified him as a master of apes. The fifth baboon bared his teeth and hissed savagely.

Instantly, the master of apes yanked back on his leash and said, "There, Hercules! There, sirrah! What do you do? What do you say?"

The baboon drew himself up and bowed curtly. "Please come with us," he said with difficulty. The master of apes cleared his throat. Sullenly, the baboon added, "Sir."

"This is outrageous!" Surplus cried. "I am a diplomat, and under international law immune to arrest."

"Ordinarily, sir, this is true," said the master of apes courteously. "However, you have entered the inner circle without her majesty's invitation and are thus subject to stricter standards of security."

"I had no idea these stairs went inward. I was led here by—" Surplus looked about helplessly. Lord Campbell-Supercollider was nowhere to be seen.

So, once again, Surplus and Darger found themselves escorted to the Office of Protocol.

ᕉᕉᕉ

"THE WOOD IS teak. Its binomial is Tectona grandis. Teak is native to Burma, Hind, and Siam. The box is carved elaborately but without refinement." The dwarf savant opened it. "Within the casing is an archaic device for electronic intercommunication. The instrument chip is a gallium-arsenide ceramic. The chip weighs six ounces. The device is a product of the Utopian end-times."

"A modem!" The protocol officer's eyes bugged out. "You dared bring a modem into the inner circle and almost into the presence of the queen?" His chair stood and walked around the table. Its six insectile legs looked too slender to carry his great, legless mass. Yet it moved nimbly and well.

"It is harmless, sir. Merely something our technarchaeologists unearthed and thought would amuse the Duke of Muscovy, who is well known for his love of all things antiquarian. It is, apparently, of some cultural or historical significance, though without rereading my instructions, I would be hard pressed to tell you what."

Lord Coherence-Hamilton raised his chair so that he loomed over Surplus, looking dangerous and domineering. "Here is the historic significance of your modem: The Utopians filled the world with their computer webs and nets, burying cables and nodes so deeply and plentifully that they shall never be entirely rooted out. They then released into that virtual universe demons and mad gods. These intelligences destroyed Utopia and almost destroyed humanity as well. Only the valiant worldwide destruction of all modes of interface saved us from annihilation.

"Oh, you lackwit! Have you no history? These creatures hate us because our ancestors created them. They are still alive, though confined to their electronic netherworld, and want only a modem to extend themselves into the physical realm. Can you wonder, then, that the penalty for possessing such a device is—" he smiled menacingly—"death?"

"No, sir, it is not. Possession of a working modem is a mortal crime. This device is harmless. Ask your savant."

"Well?" the big man growled at his dwarf. "Is it functional?"

"No. It—"

"Silence." Lord Coherence-Hamilton turned back to Surplus. "You are a fortunate cur. You will not be charged with any crimes. However, while you are here, I will keep this filthy device locked away and under my control. Is that understood, Sir Bow-Wow?"

Surplus sighed. "Very well," he said. "It is only for a week, after all."

〰️

THAT NIGHT, THE Lady Pamela Coherence-Hamilton came by Surplus's room to apologize for the indignity of his arrest, of which, she assured him, she had just now learned. He invited her in. In short order they somehow found themselves kneeling face-to-face on the bed, unbuttoning each other's clothing.

Lady Pamela's breasts had just spilled delightfully from her dress when she drew back, clutching the bodice closed again, and said, "Your man is watching us."

"And what concern is that to us?" Surplus said jovially. "The poor fellow's an autistic. Nothing he sees or hears matters to him. You might as well be embarrassed by the presence of a chair."

"Even were he a wooden carving, I would his eyes were not on me."

"As you wish." Surplus clapped his paws. "Sirrah! Turn around."

Obediently, Darger turned his back. This was his first experience with his friend's astonishing success with women. How many sexual adventuresses, he wondered, might one tumble, if one's form were unique? On reflection, the question answered itself.

Behind him, he heard the Lady Pamela giggle. Then, in a voice low with passion, Surplus said, "No, leave the diamonds on."

With a silent sigh, Darger resigned himself to a long night. Since he was bored and yet could not turn to watch the pair cavorting on the bed without giving himself away, he was perforce required to settle for watching them in the mirror.

They began, of course, by doing it doggy-style.

THE NEXT DAY, Surplus fell sick. Hearing of his indisposition, Lady Pamela sent one of her autistics with a bowl of broth and then followed, herself, in a surgical mask.

Surplus smiled weakly to see her. "You have no need of that mask," he said. "By my life, I swear that what ails me is not communicable. As you doubtless know, we who have been remade are prone to endocrinological imbalance."

"Is that all?" Lady Pamela spooned some broth into his mouth, then dabbed at a speck of it with a napkin. "Then fix it. You have been very wicked to frighten me over such a trifle."

"Alas," Surplus said sadly, "I am a unique creation, and my table of endocrine balances was lost in an accident at sea. There are copies in Vermont, of course. But by the time even the swiftest schooner can cross the Atlantic twice, I fear me I shall be gone."

"Oh, dearest Surplus!" The Lady caught up his paws in her hands. "Surely there is some measure, however desperate, to be taken?"

"Well…" Surplus turned to the wall in thought. After a very long time, he turned back and said, "I have a confession to make. The modem your brother holds for me? It is functional."

"Sir!" Lady Pamela stood, gathering her skirts, and stepped away from the bed in horror. "Surely not!"

"My darling and delight, you must listen to me." Surplus glanced weakly toward the door, then lowered his voice. "Come close and I shall whisper."

She obeyed.

"In the waning days of Utopia, during the war between men and their electronic creations, scientists and engineers bent their efforts toward the creation of a modem that could be safely employed by humans. One immune from the attack of demons. One that could, indeed, compel their obedience. Perhaps you have heard of this project."

"There are rumors, but…no such device was ever built."

"Say rather that no such device was built in time. It had just barely been perfected when the mobs came rampaging through the laboratories, and the Age of the Machine was over. Some few, however, were hidden away before the last technicians were killed. Centuries later, brave researchers at the Technarchaeological Institute of Shelburne recovered six such devices and mastered the art of their use. One device was destroyed in the process. Two are kept in Burlington. The others were given to trusted couriers and sent to the three most powerful allies of the Demesne—one of which is, of course, Russia."

"This is hard to believe," Lady Pamela said wonderingly. "Can such marvels be?"

"Madame, I employed it two nights ago in this very room! Those voices your brother heard? I was speaking with my principals in Vermont. They gave me permission to extend my stay here to a fortnight."

He gazed imploringly at her. "If you were to bring me the device, I could then employ it to save my life."

Lady Coherence-Hamilton resolutely stood. "Fear nothing, then. I swear by my soul, the modem shall be yours tonight."

THE ROOM WAS lit by a single lamp which cast wild shadows whenever anyone moved, as if of illicit spirits at a witch's Sabbath.

It was an eerie sight. Darger, motionless, held the modem in his hands. Lady Pamela, who had a sense of occasion, had changed to a low-cut gown of clinging silks, dark-red as human blood. It swirled about her as she hunted through the wainscoting for a jack left unused for centuries. Surplus sat up weakly in bed, eyes half-closed, directing her. It might have been, Darger thought, an allegorical tableau of the human body being directed by its sick animal passions, while the intellect stood by, paralyzed by lack of will.

"There!" Lady Pamela triumphantly straightened, her necklace scattering tiny rainbows in the dim light.

Darger stiffened. He stood perfectly still for the length of three long breaths, then shook and shivered like one undergoing seizure. His eyes rolled back in his head.

In hollow, unworldly tones, he said, "What man calls me up from the vasty deep?" It was a voice totally unlike his own, one harsh and savage and eager for unholy sport. "Who dares risk my wrath?"

"You must convey my words to the autistic's ears," Surplus murmured. "For he is become an integral part of the modem—not merely its operator, but its voice."

"I stand ready," Lady Pamela replied.

"Good girl. Tell it who I am."

"It is Sir Blackthorpe Ravenscairn de Plus Precieux who speaks, and who wishes to talk to…" She paused.

"To his most august and socialist honor, the mayor of Burlington."

"His most august and socialist honor," Lady Pamela began. She turned toward the bed and said quizzically, "The mayor of Burlington?"

"'Tis but an official title, much like your brother's, for he who is in fact the spy-master for the Demesne of Western Vermont," Surplus said weakly. "Now repeat to it: I compel thee on threat of dissolution to carry my message. Use those exact words."

Lady Pamela repeated the words into Darger's ear.

He screamed. It was a wild and unholy sound that sent the Lady skittering away from him in a momentary panic. Then, in mid-cry, he ceased.

"Who is this?" Darger said in an entirely new voice, this one human. "You have the voice of a woman. Is one of my agents in trouble?"

"Speak to him now, as you would to any man: forthrightly, directly, and without evasion." Surplus sank his head back on his pillow and closed his eyes.

So (as it seemed to her) the Lady Coherence-Hamilton explained Surplus's plight to his distant master, and from him received both condolences and the needed information to return Surplus's endocrine levels to a functioning harmony. After proper courtesies, then, she thanked the American spy-master and unjacked the modem. Darger returned to passivity.

The leather-cased endocrine kit lay open on a small table by the bed. At Lady Pamela's direction, Darger began applying the proper patches to various places on Surplus's body. It was not long before Surplus opened his eyes.

"Am I to be well?" he asked and, when the Lady nodded, "Then I fear I must be gone in the morning. Your brother has spies everywhere. If he gets the least whiff of what this device can do, he'll want it for himself."

Smiling, Lady Pamela hoisted the box in her hand. "Indeed, who can blame him? With such a toy, great things could be accomplished."

"So he will assuredly think. I pray you, return it to me."

She did not. "This is more than just a communication device, sir," she said. "Though in that mode it is of incalculable value. You have shown that it can enforce obedience on the creatures that dwell in the forgotten nerves of the ancient world. Ergo, they can be compelled to do our calculations for us."

"Indeed, so our technarchaeologists tell us. You must—"

"We have created monstrosities to perform the duties that were once done by machines. But with this, there would be no necessity to do so. We have allowed ourselves to be ruled by an icosahexadexal-brained freak. Now we have no need for

Gloriana the Gross, Gloriana the Fat and Grotesque, Gloriana the Maggot Queen."

"Madame!"

"It is time, I believe, that England had a new queen. A human queen."

"Think of my honor!"

Lady Pamela paused in the doorway. "You are a very pretty fellow indeed. But with this, I can have the monarchy and keep such a harem as will reduce your memory to that of a passing and trivial fancy."

With a rustle of skirts, she spun away.

"Then I am undone!" Surplus cried, and fainted onto the bed.

Quietly, Darger closed the door. Surplus raised himself from the pillows, began removing the patches from his body, and said, "Now what?"

"Now we get some sleep," Darger said. "Tomorrow will be a busy day."

ℒℛℰ

THE MASTER OF apes came for them after breakfast, and marched them to their usual destination. By now Darger was beginning to lose track of exactly how many times he had been in the Office of Protocol. They entered to find Lord Coherence-Hamilton in a towering rage, and his sister, calm and knowing, standing in a corner with her arms crossed, watching. Looking at them both now, Darger wondered how he could ever have imagined that the brother outranked his sister.

The modem lay opened on the dwarf-savant's desk. The little fellow leaned over the device, studying it minutely.

Nobody said anything until the master of apes and his baboons had left. Then Lord Coherence-Hamilton roared, "Your modem refuses to work for us!"

"As I told you, sir," Surplus said coolly, "it is inoperative."

"That's a bold-arsed fraud and a goat-buggering lie!" In his wrath, the Lord's chair rose up on its spindly legs so high that his head almost bumped against the ceiling. "I know of your activities—" he nodded toward his sister—"and demand that you show us how this whoreson device works!"

"Never!" Surplus cried stoutly. "I have my honor, sir."

"Your honor, too scrupulously insisted upon, may well lead to your death, sir."

Surplus threw back his head. "Then I die for Vermont!"

At this moment of impasse, Lady Hamilton stepped forward between the two antagonists to restore peace. "I know what might change your mind." With a knowing smile, she raised a hand to her throat and denuded herself of her diamonds. "I saw how you rubbed them against your face the other night. How you licked and fondled them. How ecstatically you took them into your mouth."

She closed his paws about them. "They are yours, sweet 'Sieur, Precieux, for a word."

"You would give them up?" Surplus said, as if amazed at the very idea. In fact, the necklace had been his and Darger's target from the moment they'd seen it. The only barrier that now stood between them and the merchants of Amsterdam was the problem of freeing themselves from the Labyrinth before their marks finally realized that the modem was indeed a cheat. And to this end they had the invaluable tool of a thinking man whom all believed to be an autistic, and a plan that would give them almost twenty hours in which to escape.

"Only think, dear Surplus." Lady Pamela stroked his head and then scratched him behind one ear, while he stared down at the precious stones. "Imagine the life of wealth and ease you could lead, the women, the power. It all lies in your hands. All you need do is close them."

Surplus took a deep breath. "Very well," he said. "The secret lies in the condenser, which takes a full day to recharge. Wait but—"

"Here's the problem," the savant said unexpectedly. He poked at the interior of the modem. "There was a wire loose."

He jacked the device into the wall.

"Oh, dear God," Darger said.

A savage look of raw delight filled the dwarf savant's face, and he seemed to swell before them.

"I am free!" he cried in a voice so loud it seemed impossible that it could arise from such a slight source. He shook as if an enormous electrical current were surging through him. The stench of ozone filled the room.

He burst into flames and advanced on the English spy-master and her brother.

While all stood aghast and paralyzed, Darger seized Surplus by the collar and hauled him out into the hallway, slamming the door shut as he did.

༄

THEY HAD NOT run twenty paces down the hall when the door to the Office of Protocol exploded outward, sending flaming splinters of wood down the hallway.

Satanic laughter boomed behind them.

Glancing over his shoulder, Darger saw the burning dwarf, now blackened to a cinder, emerge from a room engulfed in flames, capering and dancing. The modem, though disconnected, was now tucked under one arm, as if it were exceedingly valuable to him. His eyes were round and white and lidless. Seeing them, he gave chase.

"Aubrey!" Surplus cried. "We are headed the wrong way!"

It was true. They were running deeper into the Labyrinth, toward its heart, rather than outward. But it was impossible to turn back now. They plunged through scattering crowds of nobles and servitors, trailing fire and supernatural terror in their wake.

The scampering grotesque set fire to the carpets with every footfall. A wave of flame tracked him down the hall, incinerating tapestries and wallpaper and wood trim. No matter how they dodged, it ran straight toward them. Clearly, in the programmatic literalness of its kind, the demon from the web had determined that having early seen them, it must early kill them as well.

Darger and Surplus raced through dining rooms and salons, along balconies and down servants' passages. To no avail. Dogged by their hyper-natural nemesis, they found themselves running down a passage, straight toward two massive bronze doors, one of which had been left just barely ajar. So fearful were they that they hardly noticed the guards.

"Hold, sirs!"

The mustachioed master of apes stood before the doorway, his baboons straining against their leashes. His eyes widened with recognition. "By gad, it's you!" he cried in astonishment.

"Lemme kill 'em!" one of the baboons cried. "The lousy bastards!" The others growled agreement.

Surplus would have tried to reason with them, but when he started to slow his pace, Darger put a broad hand on his back and shoved. "Dive!" he commanded. So of necessity the dog of rationality had to bow to the man of action. He tobogganed wildly across the polished marble floor between two baboons, straight at the master of apes, and then between his legs.

The man stumbled, dropping the leashes as he did.

The baboons screamed and attacked.

For an instant all five apes were upon Darger, seizing his limbs, snapping at his face and neck. Then the burning dwarf arrived and, finding his target obstructed, seized the nearest baboon. The animal shrieked as its uniform burst into flames.

As one, the other baboons abandoned their original quarry to fight this newcomer who had dared attack one of their own.

In a trice, Darger leaped over the fallen master of apes, and was through the door. He and Surplus threw their shoulders against its metal surface and pushed. He had one brief glimpse of the fight, with the baboons aflame, and their master's body flying through the air. Then the door slammed shut. Internal bars and bolts, operated by smoothly oiled mechanisms, automatically latched themselves.

For the moment, they were safe.

Surplus slumped against the smooth bronze, and wearily asked, "Where did you get that modem?"

"From a dealer of antiquities." Darger wiped his brow with his kerchief. "It was transparently worthless. Whoever would dream it could be repaired?"

Outside, the screaming ceased. There was a very brief silence. Then the creature flung itself against one of the metal doors. It rang with the impact.

A delicate girlish voice wearily said, "What is this noise?"

They turned in surprise and found themselves looking up at the enormous corpus of Queen Gloriana. She lay upon her pallet, swaddled in satin and lace, and abandoned by all, save her valiant (though doomed) guardian apes. A pervasive yeasty smell emanated from her flesh. Within the tremendous folds of chins by the dozens and scores was a small human face. Its mouth moved delicately and asked, "What is trying to get in?"

The door rang again. One of its great hinges gave.

Darger bowed. "I fear, madame, it is your death."

"Indeed?" Blue eyes opened wide and, unexpectedly, Gloriana laughed. "If so, that is excellent good news. I have been praying for death an extremely long time."

"Can any of God's creations truly pray for death and mean it?" asked Darger, who had his philosophical side. "I have known unhappiness myself, yet even so life is precious to me."

"Look at me!" Far up to one side of the body, a tiny arm— though truly no tinier than any woman's arm—waved feebly. "I am not God's creation, but Man's. Who would trade ten minutes of their own life for a century of mine? Who, having mine, would not trade it all for death?"

A second hinge popped. The doors began to shiver. Their metal surfaces radiated heat.

"Darger, we must leave!" Surplus cried. "There is a time for learned conversation, but it is not now."

"Your friend is right," Gloriana said. "There is a small archway hidden behind yon tapestry. Go through it. Place your hand on the left wall and run. If you turn whichever way you must to keep from letting go of the wall, it will lead you outside. You are both rogues, I see, and doubtless deserve punishment, yet I can find nothing in my heart for you but friendship."

"Madame…" Darger began, deeply moved.

"Go! My bridegroom enters."

The door began to fall inward. With a final cry of "Farewell!" from Darger and "Come on!" from Surplus, they sped away.

By the time they had found their way outside, all of Buckingham Labyrinth was in flames. The demon, however, did not emerge from the flames, encouraging them to believe that when the modem it carried finally melted down, it had been forced to return to that unholy realm from whence it came.

৩৩

THE SKY WAS red with flames as the sloop set sail for Calais. Leaning against the rail, watching, Surplus shook his head. "What a terrible sight! I cannot help feeling, in part, responsible."

"Come! Come!" Darger said. "This dyspepsia ill becomes you. We are both rich fellows, now. The Lady Pamela's diamonds will maintain us lavishly for years to come. As for London, this is far from the first fire it has had to endure. Nor will it be the last. Life is short, and so, while we live, let us be jolly."

"These are strange words for a melancholiac," Surplus said wonderingly.

"In triumph, my mind turns its face to the sun. Dwell not on the past, dear friend, but on the future that lies glittering before us."

"The necklace is worthless," Surplus said. "Now that I have the leisure to examine it, free of the distracting flesh of Lady Pamela, I see that these are not diamonds, but mere imitations." He made to cast the necklace into the Thames.

Before he could, though, Darger snatched away the stones from him and studied them closely. Then he threw back his head and laughed. "The biters bit! Well, it may be paste, but it looks valuable still. We shall find good use for it in Paris."

"We are going to Paris?"

"We are partners, are we not? Remember that antique wisdom that whenever a door closes, another opens. For every city that burns, another beckons. To France, then, and adventure! After which, Italy, the Vatican Empire, Austro-Hungary, perhaps even Russia! Never forget that we have yet to present your credentials to the Duke of Muscovy."

"Very well," Surplus said. "But when we do, I'll pick out the modem."

The Little Cat Laughed to See Such Sport

There was a season in Paris when Darger and Surplus, those two canny rogues, lived very well indeed. That was the year when the Seine shone a gentle green at night with the pillars of the stone bridges fading up into a pure and ghostly blue, for the city engineers, in obedience to the latest fashions, had made the algae and mosses bioluminescent.

Paris, unlike lesser cities, reveled in her flaws. The molds and funguses that attacked her substance had been redesigned for beauty. The rats had been displaced by a breed of particularly engaging mice. A depleted revenant of the Plague Wars yet lingered in her brothels in the form of a sexual fever that lasted but twenty-four hours before dying away, leaving one with only memories and pleasant regrets. The health service, needless to say, made no serious effort to eradicate it.

Small wonder that Darger and Surplus were as happy as two such men could be.

One such man, actually. Surplus was, genetically, a dog, though he had been remade into anthropomorphic form and intellect. But neither that nor his American origins was held against him, for it was widely believed that he was enormously wealthy.

He was not, of course. Nor was he, as so many had been led to suspect, a baron of the Demesne of Western Vermont, traveling

41

incognito in his government's service. In actual fact, Surplus and Darger were being kept afloat by an immense sea of credit while their plans matured.

"It seems almost a pity," Surplus remarked conversationally over breakfast one morning, "that our little game must soon come to fruition." He cut a slice of strawberry, laid it upon his plate, and began fastidiously dabbing it with golden dollops of Irish cream. "I could live like this forever."

"Indeed. But our creditors could not." Darger, who had already breakfasted on toast and black coffee, was slowly unwrapping a package that had been delivered just minutes before by courier. "Nor shall we require them to. It is my proud boast to have never departed a restaurant table without leaving a tip, nor a hotel by any means other than the front door."

"I seem to recall that we left Buckingham by climbing out a window into the back gardens."

"That was the queen's palace, and quite a different matter. Anyway, it was on fire. Common law absolves us of any impoliteness under such circumstances." From a lap brimming with brown paper and excelsior, Darger withdrew a gleaming chrome pistol. "Ah!"

Surplus set down his fork and said, "Aubrey, what are you doing with that grotesque mechanism?"

"Far from being a grotesque mechanism, as you put it, my dear friend, this device is an example of the brilliance of the Utopian artisans. The trigger has a built-in gene reader so that the gun could only be fired by its registered owner. Further, it was programmed so that, while still an implacable foe of robbers and other enemies of its master, it would refuse to shoot his family or friends, were he to accidentally point the gun their way and try to fire."

"These are fine distinctions for a handgun to make."

"Such weapons were artificially intelligent. Some of the best examples had brains almost the equal of yours or mine. Here. Examine it for yourself."

Surplus held it up to his ear. "Is it humming?"

But Darger, who had merely a human sense of hearing, could detect nothing. So Surplus remained unsure. "Where did it come from?" he asked.

"It is a present," Darger said. "From one Madame Mignonette d'Etranger. Doubtless she has read of our discovery in the papers, and wishes to learn more. To which end she has enclosed her card— it is bordered in black, indicating that she is a widow—annotated with the information that she will be at home this afternoon."

"Then we shall have to make the good widow's acquaintance. Courtesy requires nothing less."

CHATEAU D'ETRANGER RESEMBLED nothing so much as one of Arcimboldo's whimsical portraits of human faces constructed entirely of fruits or vegetables. It was a bioengineered viridian structure—self-cleansing, self-renewing, and even self-supporting, were one willing to accept a limited menu—such as had enjoyed a faddish popularity in the suburban Paris of an earlier decade. The columned façade was formed by a uniform line of oaks with fluted boles above plinthed and dadoed bases. The branches swept back to form a pleached roof of leafy green. Swags of vines decorated windows that were each the translucent petal of a flower delicately hinged with clamshell muscle to air the house in pleasant weather.

"Grotesque," muttered Surplus, "and in the worst of taste."

"Yet expensive," Darger observed cheerily. "And in the final analysis, does not money trump good taste?"

Madame d'Etranger received them in the orangery. All the windows had been opened, so that a fresh breeze washed through the room. The scent of orange blossoms was intoxicating. The widow herself was dressed in black, her face entirely hidden behind a dark and fashionable cloud of hair, hat, and veils. Her clothes, notwithstanding their somber purpose, were of silk, and did little to disguise the loveliness of her slim and perfect form. "Gentlemen," she said. "It is kind of you to meet me on such short notice."

Darger rushed forward to seize her black-gloved hands. "Madame, the pleasure is entirely ours. To meet such an elegant and beautiful woman, even under what appear to be tragic circumstances, is a rare privilege, and one I shall cherish always."

Madame d'Etranger tilted her head in a way that might indicate pleasure.

"Indeed," Surplus said coldly. Darger shot him a quick look.

"Tell me," Madame d'Etranger said. "Have you truly located the Eiffel Tower?"

"Yes, madame, we have," Darger said.

"After all these years…" she marveled. "However did you find it?"

"First, I must touch lightly upon its history. You know, of course, that it was built early in the Utopian era, and dismantled at its very end, when rogue intelligences attempted to reach out from the virtual realm to seize control of the human world, and humanity fought back in every way it could manage. There were many desperate actions fought in those mad years, and none more desperate than here in Paris, where demons seized control of the Tower and used it to broadcast madness throughout the city. Men fought each other in the streets. Armed forces, sent in to restore order, were reprogrammed and turned against their own commanders. Thousands died before the Tower was at last dismantled.

"I remind you of this, so that you may imagine the determination of the survivors to ensure that the Eiffel Tower would never be raised again. Today, we think only of the seven thousand three hundred tons of puddled iron of its superstructure, and of how much it would be worth on the open market. Then, it was seen as a monster, to be buried where it could never be found and resurrected."

"As indeed, for all this time, it has not. Yet now, you tell me, you have found it. How?"

"By seeking for it where it would be most difficult to excavate. By asking ourselves where such a salvage operation would be most disruptive to contemporary Paris." He nodded to Surplus, who removed a rolled map from his valise. "Have you a table?"

Madame d'Etranger clapped her hands sharply twice. From the ferny undergrowth to one end of the orangery, an enormous tortoise patiently footed forward. The top of his shell was as high as Darger's waist, and flat.

Wordlessly, Surplus unrolled the map. It showed Paris and environs.

"And the answer?" Darger swept a hand over the meandering blue river bisecting Paris. "It is buried beneath the Seine!"

For a long moment, the lady was still. Then, "My husband will want to speak with you."

With a rustle of silks, she left the room.

As soon as she was gone, Darger turned on his friend and harshly whispered, "Damn you, Surplus, your sullen and uncooperative attitude is queering the pitch! Have you forgotten how to behave in front of a lady?"

"She is no lady," Surplus said stiffly. "She is a genetically modified cat. I can smell it."

"A cat! Surely not."

"Trust me on this one. The ears you cannot see are pointed. The eyes she takes such care to hide are a cat's eyes. Doubtless the fingers within those gloves have retractable claws. She is a cat, and thus untrustworthy and treacherous."

Madame d'Etranger returned. She was followed by two apes who carried a thin, ancient man in a chair between them. Their eyes were dull; they were little better than automata. After them came a Dedicated Doctor, eyes bright, who of course watched his charge with obsessive care. The widow gestured toward her husband. "C'est Monsieur."

"Monsieur d'Etrang—" Darger began.

"Monsieur only. It's quicker," the ancient said curtly. "My widow has told me about your proposition."

Darger bowed. "May I ask, sir, how long you have?"

"Twenty-three months, seven days, and an indeterminable number of hours," the Dedicated Doctor said. "Medicine remains, alas, an inexact science."

"Damn your impudence and shut your yap!" Monsieur snarled. "I have no time to waste on you."

"I speak only the truth. I have no choice but to speak the truth. If you wish otherwise, please feel free to deprogram me, and I will quit your presence immediately."

"When I die you can depart, and not a moment before." The slight old man addressed Darger and Surplus: "I have little time, gentlemen, and in that little time I wish to leave my mark upon the world."

"Then—forgive me again, sir, but I must say it—you have surely better things to do than to speak with us, who are in essence but glorified scrap dealers. Our project will bring its patron an enormous increase in wealth. But wealth, as you surely know, does not in and of itself buy fame."

"But that is exactly what I intend to do—buy fame." A glint came into Monsieur's eyes, and one side of his mouth turned up in a mad and mirthless grin. "It is my intent to re-erect the ancient structure as the Tour d'Etranger!"

✎

"THE TROUT HAS risen to the bait," Darger said with satisfaction. He and Surplus were smoking cigars in their office. The office was the middle room of their suite, and a masterpiece of stage-setting, with desks and tables overflowing with papers, maps, and antiquarian books competing for space with globes, surveying equipment, and a stuffed emu.

"And yet, the hook is not set. He can still swim free," Surplus riposted. "There was much talk of building coffer dams of such and so sizes and redirecting so-many-millions of liters of water. And yet not so much as a penny of earnest money."

"He'll come around. He cannot coffer the Seine segment by segment until he comes across the buried beams of the Tower. For that knowledge, he must come to us."

"And why should he do that, rather than searching it out for himself?"

"Because, dear fellow, it is not to be found there. We lied."

"We have told lies before, and had them turn out to be true."

"That too is covered. Over a century ago, an eccentric Parisian published an account of how he had gone up and down the Seine with a rowboat and a magnet suspended on a long rope from a spring scale, and found nothing larger than the occasional rusted hulk of a Utopian machine. I discovered his leaflet, its pages uncut, in the Bibliothèque Nationale."

"And what is to prevent our sponsor from reading that same chapbook?"

"The extreme unlikelihood of such a coincidence, and the fact that I later dropped the only surviving copy in all the city into the Seine."

THAT SAME NIGHT Darger, who was a light sleeper, was awakened by the sound of voices in the library. Silently, he donned blouse and trousers, and then put his ear to the connecting double doors.

He could hear the cadenced rise and fall of conversation, but could not quite make out the words. More suspiciously, no light showed in the crack under or between the doors. Surplus, he knew, would not have scheduled a business appointment without consulting him. Moreover, though one of the two murmuring voices might conceivably be female, there were neither giggles nor soft, drawn-out sighs but, rather, a brisk and informational tone to their speech. The rhythms were all wrong for it to be one of Surplus's assignations.

Resolutely, Darger flung the doors open.

The only light in the office came from the moon without. It illuminated not two but only one figure—a slender one, clad in skin-tight clothes. She (for by the outline of her shadowy body, Darger judged the intruder to be female) whirled at the sound of the doors slamming. Then, with astonishing grace, she ran out onto the balcony, jumped up on its rail, and leaped into the darkness. Darger heard the woman noisily rattling up the bamboo fire escape.

With a curse, he rushed after her.

By the time Darger had reached the roof, he fully expected his mysterious intruder to be gone. But there she was, to the far end of the hotel, crouched alongside one of the chimney-pots in a wary and watchful attitude. Of her face he could see only two unblinking glints of green fire that were surely her eyes. Silhouetted as she was against a sky filled with rags and snatches of moon-bright cloud, he could make out the outline of one pert and perfect breast, tipped with a nipple the size of a dwarf cherry. He saw how her long tail lashed back and forth behind her.

For an instant, Darger was drawn up by a wholly uncharacteristic feeling of supernatural dread. Was this some imp or fiend from the infernal nether-regions? He drew in his breath.

But then the creature turned and fled. So Darger, reasoning that if it feared him then he had little to fear from it, pursued.

The imp-woman ran to the edge of the hotel and leaped. Only a short alley separated the building from its neighbor. The leap was no more than six feet. Darger followed without difficulty. Up a sloping roof she ran. Over it he pursued her.

Another jump, of another alley.

He was getting closer now. Up a terra-cotta-tiled rooftop he ran. At the ridge-line, he saw with horror his prey extend herself in a low flying leap across a gap of at least fifteen feet. She hit the far roof with a tuck, rolled, and sprang to her feet.

Darger knew his limitations. He could not leap that gap.

In a panic, he tried to stop, tripped, fell, and found himself sliding feet-first on his back down the tiled roof. The edge sped toward him. It was a fall of he-knew-not-how-many floors to the ground. Perhaps six.

Frantically, Darger flung out his arms to either side, grabbing at the tiles, trying to slow his descent by friction. The tiles bumped painfully beneath him as he skidded downward. Then the heels of his bare feet slammed into the gutter at the edge of the eaves. The guttering groaned, lurched outward—and held.

Darger lay motionless, breathing heavily, afraid to move.

He heard a thump, and then the soft sound of feet traversing the rooftop. A woman's head popped into view, upside down in his vision. She smiled.

He knew who she was, then. There were, after all, only so many cat-women in Paris. "M-madame d'Etra—"

"Shhh." She put a finger against his lips. "No names."

Nimbly, she slipped around and crouched over him. He saw now that she was clad only in a pelt of fine black fur. Her nipples were pale and naked. "So afraid!" she marveled. Then, brushing a hand lightly over him. "Yet still aroused."

Darger felt the guttering sway slightly under him and, thinking how easily this woman could send him flying downward, he shivered. It was best he did not offend her. "Can you wonder, madame? The sight of you…"

"How gallant!" Her fingers deftly unbuttoned his trousers, and undid his belt. "You do know how to pay a lady a compliment."

"What are you doing?" Darger cried in alarm.

She tugged the belt free, tossed it lightly over the side of the building. "Surely your friend has explained to you that cats are amoral?" Then, when Darger nodded, she ran her fingers up under his blouse, claws extended, drawing blood. "So you will understand that I mean nothing personal by this."

ᘒᕄᘒ

SURPLUS WAS WAITING when Darger climbed back in the window. "Dear God, look at you," he cried. "Your clothes are dirty and disordered, your hair is in disarray—and what has happened to your belt?"

"Some mudlark of the streets has it, I should imagine." Darger sank down into a chair. "At any rate, there's no point looking for it."

"What in heaven's name has happened to you?"

"I fear I've fallen in love," Darger said sadly, and could be compelled to say no more.

SO BEGAN AN affair that seriously tried the friendship of the two partners in crime. For Madame d'Etranger thenceforth appeared in their rooms, veiled yet unmistakable, every afternoon. Invariably, Darger would plant upon her hand the chastest of kisses, and then discretely lead her to the secrecy of his bedroom, where their activities could only be guessed at. Invariably, Surplus would scowl, snatch up his walking stick, and retire to the hallway, there to pace back and forth until the lady finally departed. Only rarely did they speak of their discord.

One such discussion was occasioned by Surplus's discovery that Madame d'Etranger had employed the services of several of Paris's finest book scouts.

"For what purpose?" Darger asked negligently. Mignonette had left not half an hour previously, and he was uncharacteristically relaxed.

"That I have not been able to determine. These book scouts are a notoriously close-mouthed lot."

"The acquisition of rare texts is an honorable hobby for many haut-bourgeois."

"Then it is one she has acquired on short notice. She was unknown in the Parisian book world a week ago. Today she is one of its best patrons. Think, Darger—think! Abrupt changes of behavior are always dangerous signs. Why will you not take this seriously?"

"Mignonette is, as they say here, une chatte sérieuse, and I un homme galant." Darger shrugged. "It is inevitable that I should be besotted with her. Why cannot you, in your turn, simply accept this fact?"

Surplus chewed on a knuckle of one paw. "Very well—I will tell you what I fear. There is only one work of literature she could possibly be looking for, and that is the chapbook proving that the Eiffel Tower does not lie beneath the Seine."

"But, my dear fellow, how could she possibly know of its existence?"

"That I cannot say."

"Then your fears are groundless." Darger smiled complacently. Then he stroked his chin and frowned. "Nevertheless, I will have a word with her."

ᘏᗢᘏ

THE VERY NEXT day he did so.

The morning had been spent, as usual, in another round of the interminable negotiations with Monsieur's business agents, three men of such negligible personality that Surplus privately referred to them as Ci, Ça, and l'Autre. They were drab and lifeless creatures who existed, it sometimes seemed, purely for the purpose of preventing an agreement of any sort from coming to fruition. "They are waiting to be bribed," Darger explained when Surplus took him aside to complain of their recalcitrance.

"Then they will wait forever. Before we can begin distributing banknotes, we must first receive our earnest money. The pump must be primed. Surely even such dullards as Ci, Ça, and l'Autre can understand that much."

"Greed has rendered them impotent. Just as a heart can be made to beat so fast that it will seize up, so too here. Still, with patience I believe they can be made to see reason."

"Your patience, I suspect, is born of long afternoons and rumpled bed sheets."

Darger merely looked tolerant.

Yet it was not patience that broke the logjam, but its opposite. For that very morning, Monsieur burst into the conference room, carried in a chair by his apes and accompanied by his Dedicated Doctor. "It has been weeks," he said without preamble. "Why are the papers not ready?"

Ci, Ça, and l'Autre threw up their hands in dismay.

"The terms they require are absurd, to say the…"

"No sensible businessman would…"

"They have yet to provide any solid proof of their…"

"No, and in their position, neither would I. Popotin—" he addressed one of his apes—"the pouch."

Popotin slipped a leather pouch from his shoulder and clumsily held it open. Monsieur drew out three handwritten sheets of paper and threw them down on the table. "Here are my notes," he said. "Look them over and then draw them up in legal form." The cries of dismay from Ci, Ça, and l'Autre were quelled with one stern glare. "I expect them to be complete within the week."

Surplus, who had quickly scanned the papers, said, "You are most generous, Monsieur. The sum on completion is nothing short of breathtaking." Neither he nor Darger expected to collect that closing sum, of course. But they were careful to draw attention away from the start-up monies (a fraction of the closing sum, though by their standards enormous), that were their true objective.

Monsieur snorted. "What matter? I will be dead by then."

"I see that the Tour d'Etranger is to be given to the City of Paris," Darger said. "That is very generous of you, Monsieur. Many a man in your position would prefer to keep such a valuable property in their family."

"Eh? What family?"

"I speak, sir, of your wife."

"She will be taken care of."

"Sir?" Darger, who was sensitive to verbal nuance, felt a cold tingling at the back of his neck, a premonition of something significant being left unspoken. "What does that mean?"

"It means just what I said." Monsieur snapped his fingers to catch his apes' attention. "Take me away from here."

WHEN DARGER GOT back to his rooms, Mignonette was already waiting there. She lounged naked atop his bed, playing with the chrome revolver she had sent him before ever they had met. First she cuddled it between her breasts. Then she brought it to her mouth, ran her pink tongue up the barrel, and briefly closed her lips about its very tip. He found the sight disturbingly arousing.

"You should be careful," Darger said. "That's a dangerous device."

"Pooh! Monsieur had it programmed to defend me as well as himself." She placed the muzzle against her heart, and pulled the trigger. Nothing happened. "See? It will not fire at either of us." She handed it to him. "Try it for yourself."

With a small shudder of distaste, Darger placed the gun on a table at some distance from the bed. "I have a question to ask you," he said.

Mignonette smiled in an amused way. She rolled over on her stomach, and rose up on her knees and elbows. Her long tail moved languidly. Her cat's eyes were green as grass. "Do you want your answer now," she asked, "or later?"

Put that way, the question answered itself.

So filled with passion was Darger that he had no memory of divesting himself of his clothing, or joining Mignonette on the bed. He only knew that he was deep inside her, and that that was where he wanted to be. Her fur was soft and sleek against his skin.

THE LITTLE CAT LAUGHED TO SEE SUCH SPORT ℘ 55

It tickled him ever so slightly—just enough to be perverse, but not enough to be undesirable. Fleetingly, he felt like a zoophile, and then, even more fleetingly, realized that this must be very much like what Surplus's lady-friends experienced. But he abandoned that line of thought quickly.

Like any properly educated man of his era, Darger was capable of achieving orgasm three or four times in succession without awkward periods of detumescence in between. With Mignonette, he could routinely bring that number up to five. Today, for the first time, he reached seven.

"You wanted to ask me a question?" Mignonette said, when they were done. She lay within the crook of his arm, her cold nose snuggled up against his neck. Playfully, she put her two hands, claws sheathed, against his side and kneaded him, as if she were a true, unmodified cat.

"Hmm? Ah! Yes." Darger felt wonderfully, gloriously relaxed. He doubted he would ever move again. It took an effort for him to focus his thoughts. "I was wondering…exactly what your husband meant when he said that he would have you 'taken care of,' after his death."

"Oh." She drew away from him, and sat up upon her knees. "That. I thought you were going to ask about the pamphlet."

Again, a terrible sense of danger overcame Darger. He was extremely sensitive to such influences. It was an essential element of his personality. "Pamphlet?" he said lightly.

"Yes, that silly little thing about a man in a rowboat. Vingt Ans…something like that. I've had my book scouts scouring the stalls and garrets for it since I-forget-when."

"I had no idea you were looking for such a thing."

"Oh, yes," she said. "I was looking for it. And I have found it too."

"You have what?"

The outer doors of their apartments slammed open, and the front room filled with voices. Somebody—it could only be Monsieur—was shouting at the top of his weak voice. Surplus was clearly trying to soothe him. The Dedicated Doctor was there as well, urging his client to calm himself.

Darger leapt from the bed, and hastily threw on his clothes. "Wait here," he told Mignonette. Having some experience in matters of love, he deftly slipped between the doors without opening them wide enough to reveal her presence.

He stepped into absolute chaos.

Monsieur stood in the middle of the room waving a copy of an ancient pamphlet titled Vingt Ans dans un Bateau à Rames in the air. On its cover was a crude drawing of a man in a rowboat holding a magnet from a fishing pole. He shook it until it rattled. "Swindlers!" he cried. "Confidence tricksters! Deceivers! Oh, you foul creatures!"

"Please, sir, consider your leucine aminopeptidases," the Dedicated Doctor murmured. He wiped the little man's forehead with a medicated cloth. "You'll put your inverse troponin ratio all out of balance. Please sit down again."

"I am betrayed!"

"Sir, consider your blood pressure."

"The Tour d'Etranger was to be my immortality!" Monsieur howled. "What can such false cozeners as you know of immortality?"

"I am certain there has been a misunderstanding," Surplus said.

"Consider your fluoroimmunohistochemical systems. Consider your mitochondrial refresh rate."

The two apes, released from their chair-carrying chore, were running in panicked circles. One of them brushed against a lamp and sent it crashing to the floor.

It was exactly the sort of situation that Darger was best in. Thinking swiftly, he took two steps into the room and in an authoritative voice cried, "If you please!"

Silence. Every eye was upon him.

Smiling sternly, Darger said. "I will not ask for explanations. I think it is obvious to all of us what has happened. How Monsieur has come to misunderstand the import of the chapbook I cannot understand. But if, sir, you will be patient for the briefest moment, all will be made clear to you." He had the man! Monsieur was so perfectly confused (and anxious to be proved wrong, to boot) that he would accept anything Darger told him. Even the Dedicated Doctor was listening. Now he had but to invent some plausible story—for him a trifle—and the operation was on track again. "You see, there is—"

Behind him, the doors opened quietly. He put a hand over his eyes.

Mignonette d'Etranger entered the room, fully dressed, and carrying the chrome revolver. In her black silks, she was every inch the imperious widow. (Paradoxically, the fact that she obviously wore nothing beneath those silks only made her all the more imposing.) But she had thrown her veils back to reveal her face: cold, regal, and scornful.

"You!" She advanced wrathfully on her husband. "How dare you object to my taking a lover? How dare you!"

"You...you were..." The little man looked bewildered by her presence.

"I couldn't get what I need at home. It was only natural that I should look for it elsewhere. So it costs you a day of your life every time we make love! Aren't I worth it? So it costs you three days to tie me up and whip me! So what? Most men would die for the privilege."

She pressed the gun into his hands.

"If I mean so little to you," she cried histrionically, "then kill me!" She darted back and struck a melodramatic pose alongside Darger. "I will die beside the man I love!"

"Yes…" Belated comprehension dawned upon Monsieur's face, followed closely by a cruel smile. "The man you love."

He pointed the pistol at Darger and pulled the trigger.

But in that same instant, Mignonette flung herself before her lover, as if to shelter his body with her own. In the confines of so small a room, the gun's report was world-shattering. She spun around, clutched her bosom, and collapsed in the bedroom doorway. Blood seeped onto the carpet from beneath her.

Monsieur held up the gun and stared at it with an expression of total disbelief.

It went off again.

He collapsed dead upon the carpet.

THE POLICE NATURALLY suspected the worst. But a dispassionate exposition of events by the Dedicated Doctor, a creature compulsively incapable of lying, and an unobtrusive transfer of banknotes from Surplus allayed all suspicions. Monsieur d'Etranger's death was obviously an accident d'amour, and Darger and Surplus but innocent bystanders. With heartfelt expressions of condolence, the officers left.

When the morticians came to take away Monsieur's body, the Dedicated Doctor smiled. "What a horrible little man he was!" he exclaimed. "You cannot imagine what a relief it is to no longer give a damn about his health." He had signed death warrants for both Monsieur and his widow, though his examination of her had been cursory at best. He hadn't even touched the body.

Darger roused himself from his depressed state to ask, "Will you be returning for Madame d'Etranger's body?"

"No," the Dedicated Doctor said. "She is a cat, and therefore the disposition of her corpse is a matter for the department of sanitation."

Darger turned an ashen white. But Surplus deftly stepped beside him and seized the man's wrists in his own powerful paws. "Consider how tenuous our position is here," he murmured. Then the door closed, and they were alone again. "Anyway—what body?"

Darger whirled. Mignonette was gone.

✿✿✿

"BETWEEN THE MONEY I had to slip to les flics in order to get them to leave as quickly as they did," Surplus told his morose companion, "and the legitimate claims of our creditors, we are only slightly better off than we were when we first arrived in Paris."

This news roused Darger from his funk. "You have paid off our creditors? That is extremely good to hear. Wherever did you get that sort of money?"

"Ci, Ça, and l'Autre. They wished to be bribed. So I let them buy shares in the salvage enterprise at a greatly reduced rate. You cannot imagine how grateful they were."

It was evening, and the two associates were taking a last slow stroll along the luminous banks of the Seine. They were scheduled to depart the city within the hour via river-barge, and their emotions were decidedly mixed. No man leaves Paris entirely happily.

They came to a stone bridge, and walked halfway across it. Below, they could see their barge awaiting them. Darger opened his Gladstone and took out the chrome pistol that had been so central in recent events. He placed it on the rail. "Talk," he said.

The gun said nothing.

He nudged it ever so slightly with one finger. "It would take but a flick of the wrist to send you to the bottom of the river. I don't know if you'd rust, but I am certain you cannot swim."

"All right, all right!" the pistol said. "How did you know?"

"Monsieur had possession of an extremely rare chapbook which gave away our scheme. He can only have gotten it from one of Mignonette's book scouts. Yet there was no way she could have known of its importance—unless she had somehow planted a spy in our midst. That first night, when she broke into our rooms, I heard voices. It is obvious now that she was talking with you."

"You are a more intelligent man than you appear."

"I'll take that for a compliment. Now tell me—what was this ridiculous charade all about?"

"How much do you know already?"

"The first bullet you fired lodged in the back wall of the bedroom. It did not come anywhere near Mignonette. The blood that leaked from under her body was bull's blood, released from a small leather bladder she left behind her. After the police departed, she unobtrusively slipped out the bedroom window. Doubtless she is a great distance away by now. I know all that occurred. What I do not understand is why."

"Very well. Monsieur was a vile old man. He did not deserve a beautiful creature like Mignonette."

"On this we are as one. Go on."

"But, as he had her made, he owned her. And as she was his property, he was free to do with her as he liked." Then, when Darger's face darkened, "You misapprehend me, sir! I do not speak of sexual or sadomasochistic practices but of chattel slavery. Monsieur was, as I am sure you have noted for yourself, a possessive man. He had left instructions that upon his death, his house was to be set afire, with Mignonette within it."

"Surely, this would not be legal!"

"Read the law," the gun said. "Mignonette determined to find her way free. She won me over to her cause, and together we hatched the plan you have seen played to fruition."

"Tell me one thing," Surplus said curiously. "You were programmed not to shoot your master. How then did you manage…?"

"I am many centuries old. Time enough to hack any amount of code."

"Ah," said Surplus, in a voice that indicated he was unwilling to admit unfamiliarity with the gun's terminologies.

"But why me?" Darger slammed a hand down on the stone rail. "Why did Madame d'Etranger act out her cruel drama with my assistance, rather than…than…with someone else's?"

"Because she is a cold-hearted bitch. Also, she found you attractive. For a whore such as she, that is justification enough for anything."

Darger flushed with anger. "How dare you speak so of a lady?"

"She abandoned me," the gun said bitterly. "I loved her, and she abandoned me. How else should I speak of her under such circumstances?"

"Under such circumstances, a gentleman would not speak of her at all," Surplus said mildly. "Nevertheless, you have, as required, explained everything. So we shall honor our implicit promise by leaving you here to be found by the next passer-by. A valuable weapon such as yourself will surely find another patron with ease. A good life to you, sir."

"Wait!"

Surplus quirked an eyebrow. "What is it?" Darger asked.

"Take me with you," the gun pleaded. "Do not leave me here to be picked up by some cutpurse or bourgeois lout. I am neither a criminal nor meant for a sedentary life. I am an adventurer, like yourselves! I can be of enormous aid to you, and an invaluable prop for your illicit schemes."

Darger saw how Surplus's ears perked up at this. Quickly, and in his coldest possible manner, he said, "We are not of the same social class, sir."

Taking his friend's arm, he turned away.

Below, at the landing-stage, their barge awaited, hung with loops of fairy-lights. They descended and boarded. The hawsers were cast off, the engine fed an extra handful of sugar to wake it to life, and they motored silently down-river, while behind them the pistol's frantic cries faded slowly in the warm Parisian night. It was not long before the City of Light was a luminous blur on the horizon, like the face of one's beloved seen through tears.

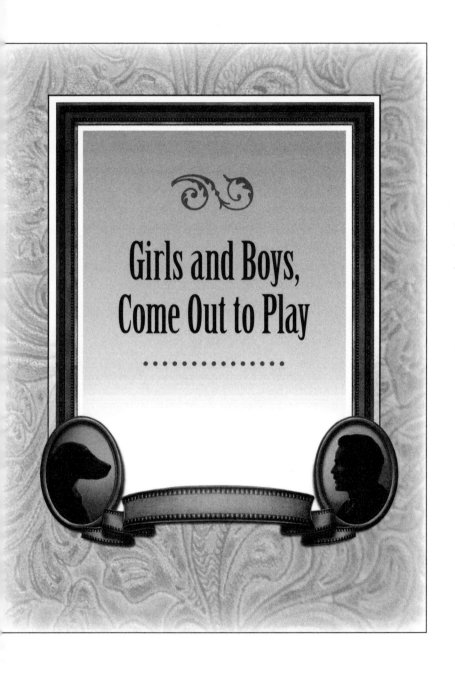

Girls and Boys,
Come Out to Play

On a hilltop in Arcadia, Darger sat talking with a satyr.

"Oh, the sex is good," the satyr said. "Nobody could say it wasn't. But is it the be-all and end-all of life? I don't see that." The satyr's name was Demetrios Papatragos, and evenings he played the saxophone in a local jazz club.

"You're a bit of a philosopher," Darger observed.

"Oh, well, in a home-grown front porch sense, I suppose I am." The satyr adjusted the small leather apron that was his only item of clothing. "But enough about me. What brings you here? We don't get that many travelers these days. Other than the African scientists, of course."

"Of course. What are the Africans here for, anyway?"

"They are building gods."

"Gods! Surely not! Whatever for?"

"Who can fathom the ways of scientists? All the way from Greater Zimbabwe they came, across the wine-dark Mediterranean and into these romance-haunted hills, and for what? To lock themselves up within the ruins of the Monastery of St. Vasilios, where they labor as diligently and joylessly as if they were indeed monks. They never come out, save to buy food and wine or to take the occasional blood sample or skin scraping. Once, one of them offered a nymph money to have sex with him, if you can believe such a thing."

"Scandalous!" Nymphs, though they were female satyrs, had neither hoofs nor horns. They were, however, not cross-fertile with humans. It was the only way, other than a small tail at the base of their spines (and that was normally covered by their dresses), to determine their race. Needless to say, they were as wildly popular with human men as their male counterparts were with women. "Sex is either freely given or it is nothing."

"You're a bit of a philosopher yourself," Papatragos said. "Say—a few of our young ladies might be in heat. You want me to ask around?"

"My good friend Surplus, perhaps, would avail himself of their kind offers. But not I. Much though I'd enjoy the act, I'd only feel guilty afterwards. It is one of the drawbacks of having a depressive turn of mind."

So Darger made his farewells, picked up his walking stick, and sauntered back to town. The conversation had given him much to think about.

ᡐᡊᡌ

"WHAT WORD OF the Evangelos bronzes?" Surplus asked. He was sitting at a table out back of their inn, nursing a small glass of retsina and admiring the sunset. The inn stood at the outskirts of town at the verge of a forest, where pine, fir, and chestnut gave way to orchards, olive trees, cultivated fields, and pastures for sheep and goats. The view from its garden could scarce be improved upon.

"None whatsoever. The locals are happy to recommend the ruins of this amphitheater or that nuclear power plant, but any mention of bronze lions or a metal man causes them only to look blank and shake their heads in confusion. I begin to suspect that scholar in Athens sold us a bill of goods."

"The biters bit! Well, 'tis an occupational hazard in our line of business."

"Sadly true. Still, if the bronzes will not serve us in one manner, they shall in another. Does it not strike you as odd that two such avid antiquarians as ourselves have yet to see the ruins of St. Vasilios? I propose that tomorrow we pay a courtesy visit upon the scientists there."

Surplus grinned like a hound—which he was not, quite. He shook out his lace cuffs and, seizing his silver-knobbed cane, stood. "I look forward to making their acquaintance."

"The locals say that they are building gods."

"Are they really? Well, there's a market for everything, I suppose."

Their plans were to take a strange turn, however. For that evening Dionysus danced through the town.

Darger was writing a melancholy letter home when the first shouts sounded outside his room. He heard cries of "Pan! Great Pan!" and wild skirls of music. Going to the window, he saw an astonishing sight: The townsfolk were pouring into the street, shedding their clothes, dancing naked in the moonlight for all to see. At their head was a tall, dark figure who pranced and leaped, all the while playing the pipes.

He got only a glimpse, but its effect was riveting. He felt the god's passage as a physical thing. Stiffening, he gripped the windowsill with both hands, and tried to control the wildness that made his heart pound and his body quiver.

But then two young women, one a nymph and the other Theodosia, the innkeeper's daughter, burst into his room and began kissing his face and urging him toward the bed.

Under normal circumstances, he would have sent them packing—he hardly knew the ladies. But the innkeeper's daughter and her goat-girl companion were both laughing and blushing so charmingly and were furthermore so eager to grapple that it seemed a pity to disappoint them. Then, too, the night was rapidly filling with the sighs and groans of human passion—no adult, apparently, was immune to the god's influence—and it seemed to Darger perverse that he alone in all the world should refuse to give in to pleasure.

So, protesting insincerely, he allowed the women to crowd him back onto the bed, to remove his clothing, and to have their wicked way with him. Nor was he backwards with them. Having once set his mind to a task, he labored at it with a will.

In a distant corner of his mind, he heard Surplus in the room down the hall raise his voice in an ecstatic howl.

DARGER SLEPT LATE the next morning. When he went down to breakfast, Theodosia was all blushes and shy smiles. She brought him a platter piled high with food, gave him a fleet peck on the cheek, and then fled happily back into the kitchen.

Women never ceased to amaze Darger. One might make free of their bodies in the most intimate manner possible, handling them not only lustfully but self-indulgently, and denying oneself not a single pleasure…yet it only made them like you the better afterwards. Darger was a staunch atheist. He did not believe in the existence of a benevolent and loving God who manipulated the world in order to maximize the happiness of His creations. Still, on a morning like this, he had to admit that all the evidence was against him.

Through an open doorway, he saw the landlord make a playful grab at his fat wife's rump. She pushed him away and, with a giggle, fled into the interior of the inn. The landlord followed.

Darger scowled. He gathered his hat and walking stick, and went outside. Surplus was waiting in the garden. "Your thoughts trend the same way as mine?" Darger asked.

"Where else could they go?" Surplus asked grimly. "We must have a word with the Africans."

The monastery was less than a mile distant, but the stroll up and down dusty country roads gave them both time enough to recover their savoir-faire. St. Vasilios, when they came to it, was dominated by a translucent green bubble-roof, fresh-grown to render the ruins habitable. The grounds were surrounded by an ancient stone wall. A wooden gate, latched but not locked, filled the lower half of a stone arch. Above it was a bell.

They rang.

Several orange-robed men were in the yard, unloading crated laboratory equipment from a wagon. They had the appearance and the formidable height of that handsomest of the world's peoples, the Masai. But whether they were of Masai descent or had merely incorporated Masai features into their genes, Darger could not say. The stocky, sweating wagoner looked like a gnome beside them. He cursed and tugged at his horses' harness to keep the skittish beasts from bolting.

At the sound of the bell, one of the scientists separated himself from the others and strode briskly to the gate. "Yes?" he said in a dubious tone.

"We wish to speak with the god Pan." Darger said. "We are from the government. "

"You do not look Greek."

"Not the local government, sir. The British government." Darger smiled into the man's baffled expression. "May we come in?"

\logp/

THEY WERE NOT brought to see Dionysus immediately, of course, but to the Chief Researcher. The scientist-monk led them to an office that was almost spartan in its appointments: a chair, a desk, a lamp, and nothing more. Behind the desk sat a girl who looked to be at most ten years old, reading a report by the lamp's gentle biofluorescence. She was a scrawny thing with a large and tightly cornrowed head. "Tell her you love her," she said curtly.

"I beg your pardon?" Surplus said.

"Tell her that, and then kiss her. That'll work better than any aphrodisiac I could give you. I presume that's what you came to this den of scientists for—that or poison. In which case, I recommend a stout cudgel at midnight and dumping the body in a marsh before daybreak. Poisons are notoriously uncertain. In either case, there is no need to involve my people in your personal affairs."

Taken aback, Darger said, "Ah, actually, we are here on official business."

The girl raised her head.

Her eyes were as dark and motionless as a snake's. They were not the eyes of a child but more like those of the legendary artificial intellects of the Utopian era—cold, timeless, calculating. A shudder ran through Darger's body. Her gaze was electrifying. Almost, it was terrifying.

Recovering himself, Darger said, "I am Inspector Darger, and this is my colleague, Sir Blackthorpe Ravenscairn de Plus Precieux. By birth an American, it goes without saying."

She did not blink. "What brings two representatives of Her Majesty's government here?"

"We have been despatched to search out and recover the Evangelos bronzes. Doubtless you know of them."

"Vaguely. They were liberated from London, were they not?"

"Looted, rather! Wrenched from Britain's loving arms by that dastard Konstantin Evangelos in an age when she was weak and Greece powerful, and upon the shoddiest of excuses—something about some ancient marbles that had supposedly...well, that hardly matters."

"Our mission is to find and recover them," Surplus elucidated.

"They must be valuable."

"Were you to discover them, they would be worth a king's ransom, and it would be my proud privilege to write you a promissory note for the full amount. However—" Darger coughed into his hand. "We, of course, are civil servants. The thanks of a grateful nation will be our reward."

"I see." Abruptly changing the subject, the Chief Researcher said, "Your friend—is he a chimeric mixture of human and animal genes, like the satyrs? Or is he a genetically modified dog? I ask only out of professional curiosity."

"His friend is capable of answering your questions for himself," Surplus said coldly. "There is no need to speak of him as if he were not present. I mention this only as a point of common courtesy. I realize that you are young, but—"

"I am older than you think, sirrah!" the girl-woman snapped. "There are disadvantages to having a childish body, but it heals quickly, and my brain cells—in stark contrast to your own, gentlemen—continually replenish themselves. A useful quality in a researcher." Her voice was utterly without warmth, but compelling nonetheless. She radiated a dark aura of authority. "Why do you wish to meet our Pan?"

"You have said it yourself—out of professional curiosity. We are government agents, and therefore interested in any new products Her Majesty might be pleased to consider."

The Chief Researcher stood. "I am not at all convinced that the Scientifically Rational Government of Greater Zimbabwe will want to export this technology after it has been tested and perfected. However, odder things have happened. So I will humor you. You must wear these patches, as do we." The Chief Researcher took two plastic bandages from a nearby box and showed how they should be applied. "Otherwise, you would be susceptible to the god's influence."

Darger noted how, when the chemicals from the drug-patch hit his bloodstream, the Chief Researcher's bleak charisma distinctly faded. These patches were, he decided, useful things indeed.

The Chief Researcher opened the office door, and cried, "Bast!"

The scientist who had led them in stood waiting outside. But it was not he who was summoned. Rather, there came the soft sound of heavy paws on stone, and a black panther stalked into the office. It glanced at Darger and Surplus with cool intelligence, then turned to the Chief Researcher. "Sssssoooooo…?"

"Kneel!" The Chief Researcher climbed onto the beast's back, commenting offhandedly, "These tiny legs make walking long distances tiresome." To the waiting scientist she said, "Light the way for us."

Taking a thurible from a nearby hook, the scientist led them down a labyrinthine series of halls and stairways, proceeding ever deeper into the earth. He swung the thurible at the end of its chain as he went, and the chemical triggers it released into the air activated the moss growing on the stone walls and ceiling so that they glowed brightly before them, and gently faded behind them.

It was like a ceremony from some forgotten religion, Darger reflected. First came the thurifer, swinging his censer with a pleasant near-regular clanking, then the dwarfish lady on her great cat, followed by the two congregants, one fully human and the other possessed of the head and other tokens of the noble dog. He could easily picture the scene painted upon an interior wall of an ancient pyramid. The fact that they were going to converse with a god only made the conceit that much more apt.

At last the passage opened into their destination.

It was a scene out of Piranesi. The laboratory had been retrofitted into the deepest basement of the monastery. The floors and roofs above had fallen in long ago, leaving shattered walls, topless pillars, and fragmentary buttresses. Sickly green light filtered through the translucent dome overhead, impeded by the many tendrils or roots that descended from above to anchor the dome by wrapping themselves about toppled stones or columnar stumps. There was a complexity of structure to the growths that made Darger feel as though he were standing within a monstrous jellyfish, or else one of those man-created beasts which, ages ago (or so legend had it), the Utopians had launched into the void between the stars in the hope that, eons hence, they might make contact with alien civilizations.

Scientists moved purposely through the gloom, feeding mice to their organic alembics and sprinkling nutrients into pulsing bioreactors. Everywhere, ungainly tangles of booms and cranes rose up from the floor or stuck out from high perches on the walls. Two limbs from the nearest dipped delicately downward, as if in curiosity. They moved in a strangely fluid manner.

"Oh, dear God!" Surplus cried.

Darger gaped and, all in an instant, the groping booms and cranes revealed themselves as tentacles. The round blobs they had taken at first for bases became living flesh. Eyes as large as dinner plates clicked open and focused on the two adventurers.

His senses reeled. Squids! And by his quick estimation, there were at a minimum several score of the creatures!

The Chief Researcher slid off her feline mount, and waved the inquiring tentacles away. "Remove Experiment One from its crypt," she commanded, and the creature flowed across the wall to do her bidding. It held itself upon the vertical surface by its suckered tentacles, Darger noted, but scuttled along the stone on short sharp legs like those of a hermit crab's. He understood now why the Chief Researcher was so interested in chimeras.

In very little time, two squids came skittering across the floor, a stone coffin in their conjoined tentacles. Gracefully, they laid it down. In unison, they raised their tentacles and lowered them in a grotesque imitation of a bow. Their beaks clacked repeatedly.

"They are intelligent creatures," the Chief Researcher commented. "But no great conversationalists."

To help regain his equilibrium, Darger fumbled out his pipe from a jacket pocket, and his tobacco pouch and a striking-box as well. But at the sight of this latter device, the squids squealed in alarm. Tentacles thrashing, they retreated several yards.

The Chief Researcher rounded on Darger. "Put that thing away!" Then, in a calmer tone, "We tolerate no open flames. The dome is a glycerol-based organism. It could go up at a spark."

Darger complied. But, true though the observation about the dome might be, he knew a lie when he heard one. So the creatures feared fire! That might be worth remembering.

"You wanted to meet Dionysus." The Chief Researcher laid a hand on the coffin. "He is here. Subordinate Researcher Mbutu, open it up."

Surplus raised his eyebrows, but said nothing.

The scientist pried open the coffin lid. For an instant nothing was visible within but darkness. Then a thousand black beetles poured from the coffin (both Darger and Surplus shuddered at the uncanniness of it) and fled into the shadows, revealing a naked man who sat up, blinking, as if just awakened.

"Behold the god."

Dionysus was an enormous man, easily seven feet tall when he stood and proportionately built, though he projected no sense of power at all. His head was either bald or shaven but in either case perfectly hairless. The scientist handed him a simple brown robe, and when he tied it up with a length of rope, he looked as if he were indeed a monk.

The panther, Bast, sat licking one enormous paw, ignoring the god entirely.

When Darger introduced himself and Surplus, Dionysus smiled weakly and reached out a trembling hand to shake. "It is very pleasant to meet folks from England," he said. "I have so few visitors." His brow was damp with sweat and his skin a pallid grey.

"This man is sick!" Darger said.

"It is but weariness from the other night. He needs more time with the physician scarabs to replenish his physical systems," the Chief Researcher said impatiently. "Ask your questions."

Surplus placed a paw on the god's shoulder. "You look unhappy, my friend."

"I—"

"Not to him," the dwarfish woman snapped, "to me! He is a proprietary creation and thus not qualified to comment upon himself."

"Very well," Darger said. "To begin, madam—why? You have made a god, I presume by so manipulating his endocrine system that he produces massive amounts of targeted pheromones on demand. But what is the point?"

"If you were in town last night, you must know what the point is. Dionysus will be used by the Scientifically Rational Government to reward its people with festivals in times of peace and prosperity as a reward for their good citizenship, and in times of unrest as a pacifying influence. He may also be useful in quelling riots. We shall see."

"I note that you referred to this man as Experiment One. May I presume you are building more gods?"

"Our work progresses well. More than that I cannot say."

"Perhaps you are also building an Athena, goddess of wisdom?"

"Wisdom, as you surely know, being a matter of pure reason, cannot be produced by the application of pheromones."

"No? Then a Ceres, goddess of the harvest? Or a Hephaestus, god of the forge? Possibly a Hestia, goddess of the hearth?"

The girl-woman shrugged. "By the tone of your questions, you know the answers already. Pheromones cannot compel skills, virtues, or abstractions—only emotions."

"Then reassure me, madam, that you are not building a Nemesis, goddess of revenge? Nor an Eris, goddess of discord. Nor an Ares, god of war. Nor a Thanatos, god of death. For if you were, the only reason I can imagine for your presence here would be that you did not care to test them out upon your own population."

The Chief Researcher did not smile. "You are quick on the uptake for a European."

"Young societies are prone to presume that simply because a culture is old, it must therefore be decadent. Yet it is not we who are running experiments upon innocent people without their knowledge or consent."

"I do not think of Europeans as people. Which I find takes care of any ethical dilemmas."

Darger's hand whitened on the knob of his cane. "Then I fear, madam, that our interview is over."

On the way out, Surplus accidentally knocked over a beaker. In the attendant confusion, Darger was able to surreptitiously slip a box of the anti-pheromonal patches under his coat. There was no obvious immediate use for the things. But from long experience, they both knew that such precautions often prove useful.

THE JOURNEY BACK to town was slower and more thoughtful than the journey out had been. Surplus broke the silence at last by saying, "The Chief Researcher did not rise to the bait."

"Indeed. And I could not have been any more obvious. I as good as told her that we knew where the bronzes were, and were amenable to being bribed."

"It makes one wonder," Surplus said, "if our chosen profession is not, essentially, sexual in nature."

"How so?"

"The parallels between cozening and seduction are obvious. One presents oneself as attractively as possible and then seeds the situation with small deceits, strategic retreats, and warm confidences. The desired outcome is never spoken of directly until it has been achieved, though all parties involved are painfully aware of it. Both activities are woven of silences, whispers, and meaningful looks. And—most significantly—the Chief Researcher, artificially maintained in an eternal prepubescence, appears to be immune to both."

"I think—"

Abruptly, a nymph stepped out into the road before them and stood, hands on hips, blocking their way.

Darger, quick-thinking as ever, swept off his hat and bowed deeply. "My dear miss! You must think me a dreadful person, but in all the excitement last night, I failed to discover your name. If you would be so merciful as to bestow upon me that knowledge and your forgiveness…and a smile… I would be the happiest man on earth."

A smile tugged at one corner of the nymph's mouth, but she scowled it down. "Call me Anya. But I'm not here to talk about myself, but about Theodosia. I'm used to the ways of men, but she is not. You were her first."

"You mean she was a…?" Darger asked, shocked.

"With my brothers and cousins and uncles around? Not likely! There's not a girl in Arcadia who keeps her hymen a day longer than she desires it. But you were her first human male. That's special to a lass."

"I feel honored, of course. But what is it specifically that you are asking me?"

"Just—" her finger tapped his chest—"watch it! Theodosia is a good friend of mine. I'll not have her hurt." And, so saying, she flounced back into the forest and was gone.

"Well!" Surplus said. "Further proof, if any were needed, that women remain beyond the comprehension of men."

"Interestingly enough, I had exactly this conversation with a woman friend of mine some years ago," Darger said, staring off into the green shadows, "and she assured me that women find men equally baffling. It may be that the problem lies not in gender but in human nature itself."

"But surely—" Surplus began.

So discoursing, they wended their way home.

A FEW DAYS later, Darger and Surplus were making their preparations to leave—and arguing over whether to head straight for

Moscow or to make a side-trip to Prague—when Eris, the goddess of discord, came stalking through the center of town, leaving fights and arguments in her wake.

Darger was lying fully clothed atop his bed, savoring the smell of flowers, when he heard the first angry noises. Theodosia had filled the room with vases of hyacinths as an apology because she and Anya had to drive to a nearby duck farm to pick up several new eider-down mattresses for the inn, and as a promise that they would not be over-late coming to him. He jumped up and saw the spreading violence from the window. Making a hasty grab for the box of patches they had purloined from the monastery, he slapped one on his neck.

He was going to bring a patch to Surplus's room, when the door flew open, and that same worthy rushed in, seized him, and slammed him into wall.

"You false friend!" Surplus growled. "You smiling, scheming... anthropocentrist!"

Darger could not respond. His friend's paws were about his neck, choking him. Surplus was in a frenzy, due possibly to his superior olfactory senses, and there was no hope of talking sense into him.

To Darger's lasting regret, his childhood had not been one of privilege and gentility, but spent in the rough-and-tumble slums of Mayfair. There, perforce, he had learned to defend himself with his fists. Now, for a silver lining, he found those deplorable skills useful.

Quickly, he brought up his forearms, crossed at the wrists, between Surplus's arms. Then, all in one motion, he thrust his arms outward, to force his friend's paws from his throat. Simultaneously, he brought up one knee between Surplus's legs as hard as he could.

Surplus gasped, and reflexively clutched his wounded part.

A shove sent Surplus to the floor. Darger pinned him.

Now, however, a new problem arose. Where to put the patch. Surplus was covered with fur, head to foot. Darger thought back to their first receiving the patches, twisted around one arm, and found a small bald spot just beneath the paw, on his wrist.

A motion, and it was done.

༄

"THEY'RE WORSE THAN football hooligans," Surplus commented. Somebody had dumped a wagonload of hay in the town square and set it ablaze. By its unsteady light could be seen small knots of townsfolk wandering the streets, looking for trouble and, often enough, finding it. Darger and Surplus had doused their own room's lights, so they could observe without drawing attention to themselves.

"Not so, dear friend, for such ruffians go to the matches intending trouble, while these poor souls…" His words were cut off by the rattle of a wagon on the street below.

It was Theodosia and Anya, returned from their chore. But before Darger could cry out to them, several men rushed toward them with threatening shouts and upraised fists. Alarmed, Theodosia gestured menacingly with her whip for them to keep back. But one of their number rushed forward, grabbed the whip, and yanked her off the wagon.

"Theodosia!" Darger cried in horror.

Surplus leaped to the windowsill and gallantly launched himself into space, toward the wagonload of mattresses. Darger, who had a touch of acrophobia and had once broken a leg performing a similar stunt, pounded down the stairs.

There were only five thugs in the attacking group, which explained why they were so perturbed when Darger burst from the inn, shouting and wielding his walking stick as if it were a cudgel and Surplus suddenly popped up from within the wagon, teeth bared and fur all a-hackle. Then Anya regained the whip and laid about her, left and right, with a good will.

The rioters scattered like pigeons.

When they were gone, Anya turned on Darger. "You knew something like this was going to happen!" she cried. "Why didn't you warn anybody?"

"I did! Repeatedly! You laughed in my face!"

"There is a time for lovers' spats," Surplus said firmly, "and this is not it. This young lady is unconscious; help me lift her into the wagon. We must get her out of town immediately."

৩৩

THE NEAREST PLACE of haven, Anya decided, was her father's croft, just outside town. Not ten minutes later, they were unloading Theodosia from the wagon, using one of the feather mattresses as a stretcher. A plump nymph, Anya's mother, met them at the door.

"She will be fine," the mother said. "I know these things, I used to be a nurse." She frowned. "Provided she doesn't have a concussion." She looked at Darger shrewdly. "Has this anything to do with the fire?"

But when Darger started to explain, Surplus tugged at his sleeve. "Look outside," he said. "The locals have formed a fire brigade."

Indeed, there were figures coming down the road, hurrying toward town. Darger ran out and placed himself in front of the first, a pimply-faced young satyr lugging a leather bucketful of water. "Stop!" he cried. "Go no further!"

The satyr paused, confused. "But the fires…"

"Worse than fires await you in town," Darger said. "Anyway, it's only a hay-rick."

A second bucket-carrying satyr pulled to a stop. It was Papatragos. "Darger!" he cried. "What are you doing here at my croft? Is Anya with you?"

For an instant, Darger was nonplused. "Anya is your daughter?"

"Aye." Papatragos grinned. "I gather that makes me practically your father-in-law."

By now all the satyrs who had been near enough to see the flames and had come with buckets to fight them—some twenty in all—were clustered about the two men. Hurriedly, Surplus told all that they knew of Pan, Eris and the troubles in town.

"Nor is this matter finished," Darger said. "The Chief Researcher said something about using Dionysus to stop riots. Since he has not appeared to do so tonight, that means they will have to create another set of riots to test that ability as well. More trouble is imminent."

"That is no concern of mine," said one stodgy-looking crofter.

"It will be ours," Darger declared, with his usual highhanded employment of the first person plural pronoun. "As soon as the agent of the riots has left town, she will surely show up here next. Did not Dionysus dance in the fields after he danced in the streets? Then Eris is on her way here to set brother against brother, and father against son."

Angry mutters passed among the satyrs. Papatragos held up his hands for silence. "Tragopropos!" he said to the pimply-faced satyr. "Run and gather together every adult satyr you can. Tell them to seize whatever weapons they can and advance upon the monastery."

"What of the townsfolk?"

"Somebody else will be sent for them. Why are you still standing here?"

"I'm gone!"

"The fire in town has gone out," Papatragos continued. "Which means that Eris is done her work and has left. She will be coming up this very road in not too long."

"Fortunately," Darger said, "I have a plan."

DARGER AND SURPLUS stood exposed in the moonlight at the very center of the road, while the satyrs hid in the bushes at its verge. They did not have long to wait.

A shadow moved toward them, grew, solidified, and became a goddess.

Eris stalked up the road, eyes wild and hair in disarray. Her clothes had been ripped to shreds; only a few rags hung from waist and ankles, and they hid nothing of her body at all. She made odd chirping and shrieking noises as she came, with sudden small hops to the side and leaps into the air. Darger had known all manner of madmen in his time. This went far beyond anything he had ever seen for sheer chaotic irrationality.

Spying them, Eris threw back her head and trilled like a bird. Then she came running and dancing toward the two friends, spinning about and beating her arms against her sides. Had she lacked the strength of the frenzied, she would still have been terrifying, for it was clear that she was capable of absolutely anything. As it was, she was enough to make a brave man cringe.

"Now!"

At Darger's command, every satyr stepped forward onto the road and threw his bucket of water at the goddess. Briefly, she was inundated. All her sweat—and, hopefully, her pheromones as well—was washed clear of her body.

As one, the satyrs dropped their buckets. Ten of them rushed forward with drug patches and slapped them onto her body. Put off her balance by the sudden onslaught, Eris fell to the ground.

"Now stand clear!" Darger cried.

The satyrs danced back. One who had hesitated just a bit in finding a space for his patch stayed just a little too long and was caught by her lingering pheromones. He drew back his foot to kick the prone goddess. But Papatragos darted forward to drag him out of her aura before he could do so.

"Behave yourself," he said.

Eris convulsed in the dirt, flipped over on her stomach, and vomited. Slowly, then, she stood. She looked around her dimly, wonderingly. Her eyes cleared, and an expression of horror and remorse came over her face.

"Oh, sweet science, what have I done?" she said. Then she wailed, "What has happened to my clothes?"

She tried to cover herself with her hands.

One of the young satyrs snickered, but Papatragos quelled him with a look. Surplus, meanwhile, handed the goddess his jacket. "Pray, madam, don this," he said courteously and, to the others, "Didn't one of you bring a blanket for the victims of the fire? Toss that to the lady—it'll make a fine skirt."

Somebody started forward with a blanket, then hesitated. "Is it safe?"

"The patches we gave you will protect against her influence," Darger assured him.

"Unfortunately, those were the last," Surplus said sadly. He turned the box upside down and shook it.

"The lady Eris will be enormously tired for at least a day. Have you a guest room?" Darger asked Papatragos. "Can she use it?"

"I suppose so. The place already looks like an infirmary."

At which reminder, Darger hurried inside to see how Theodosia was doing.

But when he got there, Theodosia was gone, and Anya and her mother as well. At first, Darger suspected foul play. But a quick search of the premises showed no signs of disorder. Indeed, the mattress had been removed (presumably to the wagon, which was also gone) and all the dislocations attendant upon it having been brought into the farmhouse had been tidied away. Clearly, the women had gone off somewhere, for purposes of their own. Which thought made Darger very uneasy indeed.

Meanwhile, the voices of gathering men and satyrs could be heard outside. Surplus stuck his head through the door and cleared his throat. "Your mob awaits."

ॐ

THE STREAM OF satyrs and men, armed with flails, pruning-hooks, pitchforks and torches, flowed up the mountain roads toward the Monastery of St. Vasilios. Where roads met, more crofters and townsfolk poured out of the darkness, streams merging and the whole surging onward with renewed force.

Darger began to worry about what would happen when the vigilantes reached their destination. Tugging at Surplus's sleeve, he drew his friend aside. "The scientists can escape easily enough," he said. "All they need do is flee into the woods. But I worry about Dionysus, locked in his crypt. This expedition is quite capable of torching the building."

"If I cut across the fields, I could arrive at the monastery before the vigilantes do, though not long before. It would be no great feat to slip over a back wall, force a door, and free the man."

Darger felt himself moved. "That is inutterably good of you, my friend."

"Poof!" Surplus said haughtily. "It is a nothing."

And he was gone.

◦◦◦

BY DARGER'S ESTIMATE, the vigilantes were a hundred strong by the time they reached the Monastery of St. Vasilios. The moon rode high among scattered shreds of cloud, and shone so bright that they did not need torches to see by, but only for their psychological effect. They raised a cry when they saw the ruins, and began running toward them.

Then they stopped.

The field before the monastery was alive with squids.

The creatures had been loathsome enough in the context of the laboratory. Here, under a cloud-torn sky, arrayed in regular ranks like an army, they were grotesque and terrifying. Tentacles lashing, the cephalopods advanced, and as they did so it could be seen that they held swords and pikes and other weapons, hastily forged but obviously suitable for murderous work.

Remembering, however, how they feared fire, Darger snatched up a torch and thrust it at the nearest rank of attackers. Chittering and clacking, they drew away from him. "Torches to the fore!" he cried. "All others follow in their wake!"

So they advanced, the squid-army retreating, until they were almost to St. Vasilios itself.

But an imp-like creature waited for them atop the monastery wall. It was a small black lump of a being, yet its brisk movements and rapid walk conveyed an enormous sense of vitality. There was a presence to this thing. It could not be ignored.

It was, Darger saw, the Chief Researcher.

One by one, the satyrs and men stumbled to a halt. They milled about, uneasy and uncertain, under the force of her scornful glare.

"You've come at least, have you?" The Chief Researcher strutted back and forth on the wall, as active and intimidating as a basilisk. A dark miasma seemed to radiate from her, settling upon the crowd and sapping its will. Filling them all with doubts and dark imaginings. "Doubtless you think you came of your own free will, driven by anger and self-righteousness. But you're here by my invitation. I sent you first Dionysus and then Eris to lure you to my doorstep, so that I might test the third deity of my great trilogy."

Standing at the front of the mob, Darger cried, "You cannot bluff us!"

"You think I'm bluffing?" The Chief Researcher flung out an arm toward the looming ruins behind her. "Behold my masterpiece—a god who is neither anthropomorphic nor limited to a single species, a god for humans and squids alike, a chimera stitched together from the genes of a hundred sires…" Her laughter was not in the least bit sane. "I give you Thanatos—the god of death!"

The dome of the monastery rippled and stirred. Enormous flaps of translucent flesh, like great wings, unfolded to either side, and the forward edge heaved up to reveal a lightless space from which slowly unreeled long, barb-covered tentacles.

Worse than any merely visual horror, however, was the overwhelming sense of futility and despair that now filled the world. All felt its immensely dispiriting effect. Darger, whose inclination was naturally toward the melancholic, found himself thinking of annihilation. Nor was this entirely unattractive. His thoughts turned to the Isle of the Dead, outside Venice, where the graves were twined with nightshade and wolfsbane, and yew-trees dropped their berries on the silent earth. He yearned to drink of Lethe's ruby cup, while beetles crawled about his feet, and death-moths fluttered about his head. To slip into the voluptuously accommodating bed of the soil, and there consort with the myriad who had gone before.

All around him, people were putting down their makeshift agricultural weapons. One let fall a torch. Even the squids dropped their swords and huddled in despair.

Something deep within Darger struggled to awaken. This was not, he knew, natural. The Chief Researcher's god was imposing despair upon them all against their better judgments. But, like rain from a weeping cloud, sorrow poured down over him, and he was helpless before it. All beauty must someday die, after all, and should he who was a lover of beauty survive? Perish the thought!

Beside him, a satyr slid to the ground and wept.

Alas, he simply did not care.

ᏇᎵ

SURPLUS, MEANWHILE, WAS in his element. Running headlong through the night, with the moon bouncing in the sky above, he felt his every sense to be fully engaged, fully alive. Through spinneys and over fields he ran, savoring every smell, alert to the slightest sound.

By roundabout ways he came at last to the monastery. The ground at its rear was untended and covered with scrub forest. All to the good. Nobody would see him here. He could find a back entrance or a window that might be forced and...

At that very instant, he felt a warm puff of breath on the back of his neck. His hackles rose. Only one creature could have come up behind him so silently as to avoid detection.

"Nobody's here," Bast said.

Surplus spun about, prepared to defend himself to the death. But the great cat merely sat down and began tending to the claws of one enormous paw, biting and tugging at them with fastidious care.

"Excuse me?"

"Our work now being effectively over, we shall soon return to Greater Zimbabwe. So, in the spirit of tying up all loose ends, the monks have been sent to seize the Evangelos bronzes as a gift for the Scientifically Chosen Council of Rational Governance back home. The Chief Researcher, meanwhile, is out front, preparing to deal with insurgent local rabble."

Surplus rubbed his chin thoughtfully with the knob of his cane. "Hum. Well…in any case, that is not why I am here. I have come for Dionysus."

"The crypt is empty," Bast said. "Shortly after the monks and the Chief Researcher left, an army of nymphs came and wrested the god from his tomb. If you look, you can see where they broke a door in."

"Do you know where they have taken him?" Surplus asked.

"Yes."

"Then, will you lead me there?"

"Why should I?"

Surplus started to reply, then bit his words short. Argument would not suffice with this creature—he was a cat, and cats did not respond to reason. Best, then, to appeal to his innate nature. "Because it would be a pointless and spiteful act of mischief."

Bast grinned. "They have taken him to their temple. It isn't far—a mile, perhaps less."

He turned away. Darger followed.

The temple was little more than a glen surrounded by evenly spaced slim white trees, like so many marble pillars. A small and simple altar stood to one end. But the entrance was flanked by two enormous pairs of metal lions, and off to one side stood the heroic bronze of a lordly man, three times the height of a mere mortal.

They arrived at the tail end of a small war.

The monks had arrived first and begun to set up blocks and tackle, in order to lower the bronze man to the ground. Barely had they begun their enterprise, however, when an army of nymphs arrived, with Dionysus cradled in a wagonload of feather mattresses. Their initial outrage at what they saw could only be imagined by its aftermath: Orange-robed monks fled wildly through the woods, pursued by packs of raging nymphs. Here and there, one had fallen, and the women performed abominable deeds upon their bodies.

Surplus looked resolutely away. He could feel the violent emotion possessing the women right through the soothing chemical voice of the patches he still wore, a passion that went far beyond sex into realms of fear and terror. He could not help remembering that the word "panic" was originally derived from the name Pan.

He strolled up to the wagon, and said, "Good evening, sir. I came to make sure you are well."

Dionysus looked up and smiled wanly. "I am, and I thank you for your concern." A monk's scream split the night. "However, if my ladies catch sight of you, I fear you will suffer even as many of my former associates do now. I'll do my best to calm them, but meanwhile, I suggest that you—" He looked suddenly alarmed. "Run!"

LETHARGY FILLED DARGER. His arms were leaden and his feet were unable to move. It seemed too much effort even to breathe. A listless glance around him showed that all his brave mob were incapacitated, some crouched and others weeping, in various attitudes of despair. Event the chimeric squid had collapsed into moist and listless blobs on the grass. He saw one taken up by Thanatos's tentacles, held high above the monastery, and then dropped into an unsuspected maw therein.

It did not matter. Nothing did.

Luckily, however, such sensations were nothing new to Darger. He was a depressive by humor, well familiar with the black weight of futility, like a hound sitting upon his heart. How many nights had he lain sleepless and waiting for a dawn he knew would never arrive? How many mornings had he forced himself out of bed, though he could see no point to the effort? More than he could count.

There was still a torch in his hand. Slowly, Darger made his shuffling way through the unresisting forms of his supporters. He lacked the energy to climb the wall, so he walked around it until he came to the gate, reached in to unlatch it, and then walked through.

He trudged up to the monastery.

So far, he had gone unnoticed because the men and satyrs wandered aimlessly about in their despair, and his movement had been cloaked by theirs. Within the monastery grounds, however, he was alone. The bright line traced by his torch attracted the Chief Researcher's eye.

"You!" she cried. "British government man! Put that torch down." She jumped down from the wall and trotted toward him. "It's hopeless, you know. You've already lost. You're as good as dead."

She was at his side now, and reaching for the torch. He raised it up, out of her reach.

"You don't think this is going to work, do you?" She punched and kicked him, but they were the blows of a child, and easy to ignore. "You don't honestly think there's any hope for you?"

He sighed. "No."

Then he threw the torch.

Whomp! The dome went up in flames. Light and heat filled the courtyard. Shielding his eyes, Darger looked away, to see satyrs and men staggering to their feet, and squids fluidly slipping downslope toward the river. Into the water they went and downstream, swimming with the current toward the distant Aegean.

Thanatos screamed. It was a horrid, indescribable sound, like fingernails on slate impossibly magnified, like agony made physical. Enormous tentacles slammed at the ground in agony, snatching up whatever they encountered and flinging it into the night sky.

A little aghast at what he had unleashed, Darger saw one of the tentacles seize the Chief Researcher and haul her high into the air, before catching fire itself and raining down black soot, both chimeric and human, on the upturned faces below.

AFTERWARDS, STARING AT the burning monastery from a distance, Darger murmured, "I have the most horrid sensation of déjà vu. Must all our adventures end the same way?"

"For the sake of those cities we have yet to visit, I sincerely hope not," Surplus replied.

There was a sudden surge of flesh and the great cat Bast took a seat alongside them. "She was the last of her kind," he remarked.

"Eh?" Darger said.

"No living creature remembers her name, but the Chief Researcher was born—or perhaps created—in the waning days of Utopia. I always suspected that her ultimate end was to recreate that lost and bygone world." Bast yawned vastly, his pink tongue curling into a question mark which then disappeared as his great black jaws snapped shut. "Well, no matter. With her gone, it's back to Greater Zimbabwe for the rest of us. I'll be glad to see the old place again. The food here is good, but the hunting is wretched."

With a leap, he disappeared into the night.

But now Papatragos strode up and clapped them both on the shoulders. "That was well done, lads. Very well done, indeed."

"You lied to me, Papatragos," Darger said sternly. "The Evangelos bronzes were yours all along."

Papatragos pulled an innocent face. "Why, whatever do you mean?"

"I've seen the lions and the bronze man," Surplus said. "It is unquestionably the statue of Lord Nelson himself, stolen from Trafalgar Square in ancient times by the rapacious Grecian Empire. How can you possibly justify keeping it?"

Now Papatragos looked properly abashed. "Well, we're sort of attached to the old thing. We walk past it every time we go to worship. It's not really a part of our religion, but it's been here so long, it almost feels as if it should be, you see."

"Exactly what is your religion?" Surplus asked curiously.

"We're Jewish," Papatragos said. "All satyrs are."

"Jewish?!"

"Well, not exactly Orthodox Jews." He shuffled his feet. "We couldn't be, not with these cloven hooves. But we have our rabbis and our shuls. We manage."

It was then that Dionysus began to play his panpipes and the crowd of nymphs and women from the temple flowed onto the former battleground. Surplus's ears pricked up. "Well, it seems the night will not be a total waste of time, after all," Papatragos said brightly. "Will you be staying?"

"No," Darger said, "I believe I will return to our inn to contemplate mortality and the fate of gods."

 logie

YET DARGER WAS no more than halfway back to town when he came upon a wagon piled high with feather mattresses, pulled over to the side of the road. The horses had been unharnessed so they could graze, and sweet sighs and giggles came from the top of the mattresses.

Darger stopped, appalled. He knew those sounds well, and recognized too the pink knee that stuck out here, the tawny shoulders draped with long black hair that arched up there. It was Theodosia and Anya. Together. Alone.

In an instant's blinding insight, he understood all. It was an old and familiar situation: Two women who loved each other but were too young to embrace the fact in all its implications, and so brought a third, male, partner into their dalliances. It hardly mattered who. Unless, of course, you were the unimportant male himself. In which case, it was a damnable insult.

"Who's there?" The two women pulled apart and struggled up out of the mattresses. Their heads appeared over the top of the wagon. Hair black and blond, eyes brown and green, one mouth sweet and the other sassily sticking out a little pink triangle of tongue. Both were, implicitly, laughing at him.

"Never mind about me," Darger said stiffly. "I see the way the wind blows. Continue, I pray you. I retain the fondest memories of you both, and I wish you nothing but well."

The women stared at him with frank astonishment. Then Theodosia whispered in Anya's ear, and Anya smiled and nodded. "Well?" Theodosia said to Darger. "Are you joining us or not?"

Darger wanted to spurn their offer, if for no other reason than his dignity's sake. But, being merely human—and male to boot—he complied.

SO FOR A space of time Darger and Surplus stayed in Arcadia and were content. Being the sort of men they were, however, mere contentment could never satisfy them for long, and so one day they loaded their bags into a rented pony-cart and departed. For once, though, they left behind people who genuinely regretted seeing them leave.

Some distance down the road, as they passed by the ruins of the Monastery of St. Vasilios, the pony grew restive and they heard the music of pipes.

There, sitting atop the wall, waiting for them, was Dionysus. He was wearing a peasant's blouse and trousers, but even so, he looked every inch a god. He casually set down his panpipes. "Bach," he said. "The old tunes are best, don't you agree?"

"I prefer Vivaldi," Darger said. "But for a German, Bach wasn't bad."

"So. You're leaving, are you?"

"Perhaps we'll be back, someday," Surplus said.

"I hope you're not thinking of returning for the bronzes?"

It was as if a cloud had passed before the sun. A dark shiver ran through the air. Dionysus was, Darger realized, preparing to assume his aspects of godhead should that prove necessary.

"If we were," he said, "would this be a problem?"

"Aye. I have no objection to your bronze man and his lions going home. Though the morality of their staying or returning is more properly a matter for the local rabbis to establish. Unfortunately, there would be curiosity as to their provenance and from whence they had come. This land would be the talk of the world. But I would keep our friends as obscure as possible for as long as may be. And you?"

Surplus sighed. "It is hard to put this into words. It would be a violation of our professional ethics not to return for the bronzes. And yet…"

"And yet," Darger said, "I find myself reluctant to reintroduce this timeless land to the modern world. These are gentle folk, their destruction of St. Vasilios notwithstanding, and I fear for them all. History has never been kind to gentle folk."

"I agree with you entirely. Which is why I have decided to stay and to protect them."

"Thank you. I have grown strangely fond of them all."

"I as well," Surplus said.

Dionysus leaned forward. "That is good to hear. It softens the hurt of what I must say to you. Which is: Do not return. I know what sort of men you are. A week from now, or a month, or a year, you will think again of the value of the bronzes. They are in and of themselves worth a fortune. Returned to England, the prestige they would confer upon their finders is beyond price. Perhaps you have been guilty of criminal activities; for this discovery, much would be forgiven. Such thoughts will occur to you. Think, also this: That these folk are protected not by me alone, but by the madness I can bring upon them. I want you to leave this land and never come back."

"What—never return to Arcadia?" Surplus said.

"You do not know what you ask, sir!" Darger cried.

"Let this be an Arcadia of the heart to you. All places abandoned and returned to must necessarily disappoint. Distance will keep its memory evergreen in your hearts." Now Dionysus reached out and embraced them both, drawing them to his bosom. In a murmurous voice, he said, "You need a new desire. Let me tell you of a place I glimpsed en route to Greece, back when I was merely human. It has many names, Istanbul and Constantinople not the least among them, but currently it is called Byzantium."

Then for a time he spoke of that most cosmopolitan of cities, of its mosques and minarets and holographic pleasure-gardens, of its temples and palaces and baths, where all the many races of the world met and shared their lore. He spoke of regal women as alluring as dreams, and of philosophers so subtle in their equivocations that no three could agree what day of the week it was. He spoke too of treasures: gold chalices, chess sets carved of porphyry and jade, silver-stemmed cups of narwhal ivory delicately carved with unicorns and maidens, swords whose hilts were flecked with gems and whose blades no force could shatter, tuns of wine whose intoxicating effects had been handcrafted by the finest storytellers in the East, vast libraries whose every book was the last surviving copy of its text. There was always music in the air of Byzantium, and the delicate foods of a hundred cultures, and of a summer's night, lovers gathered on the star-gazing platforms to practice the amatory arts in the velvety perfumed darkness. For the Festival of the Red and White Roses, streams and rivers were rerouted to run through the city streets, and a province's worth of flowers were plucked and their petals cast into the flowing waters. For the Festival of the Honey of Eden...

Some time later, Darger shook himself from his reverie, and discovered that Surplus was staring blindly into the distance, while their little pony stamped his feet and shook his harness, anxious to be off. He gripped his friend's shoulder. "Ho! Sleepy-head! You've wandered off into the Empyrean, when you're needed here on Earth."

Surplus shook himself. "I dreamed...what did I dream? It's lost now, and yet it seemed vitally important at the time, as if it were something I should remember, and even cherish." He yawned greatly. "Well, no matter! Our stay in the countryside has been pleasant, but unproductive. The Evangelos bronzes remain lost, and our purses are perilously close to empty. Where shall we go now, to replenish them?"

"East," Darger said decisively. "East, to the Bosporus. I have heard—somewhere—great things of that city called...called..."

"Byzantium!" Surplus said. "I too have heard wondrous tales—somehow—of its wealth and beauty. Two such men as ourselves should do marvelous well there."

"Then we are agreed." Darger shook the harness, and the pony set out at a trot. They both whooped and laughed, and if there was a small hurt in their hearts they did not know what it was or what they should do about it, and so it was ignored.

Surplus waved his tricorn hat in the air. "Byzantium awaits!"

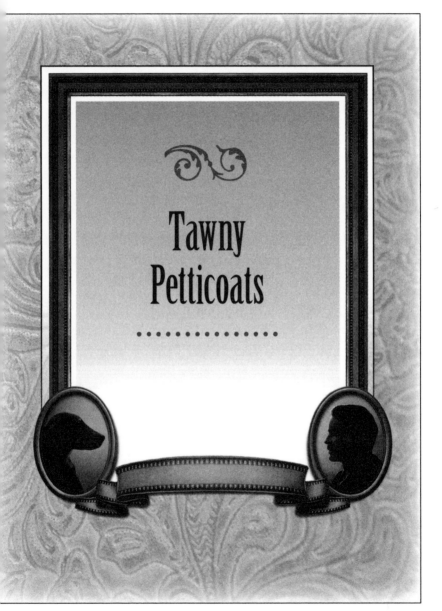

Tawny
Petticoats

The independent port city and (some said) pirate haven of New Orleans was home to many a strange sight. It was a place where sea serpents hauled ships past fields worked by zombie laborers to docks where cargo was loaded onto wooden wagons to be pulled through streets of crushed oyster shells by teams of pygmy mastodons as small as Percheron horses. So none thought it particularly noteworthy when for three days an endless line of young women waited in the hallway outside a luxury suite in the Maison Fema for the opportunity to raise their skirts or open their blouses to display a tattooed thigh, breast, or buttock to two judges who sat on twin chairs watching solemnly, asked a few questions, thanked them for their time, and then showed them out.

The women had come in response to a handbill, posted throughout several parishes, that read:

SEEKING AN HEIRESS
ARE YOU…
A YOUNG WOMAN BETWEEN THE AGES OF 18 AND 21?
FATHERLESS?
TATTOOED FROM BIRTH ON AN INTIMATE PART OF
    YOUR BODY?

IF SO, YOU MAY BE ENTITLED TO GREAT RICHES
INQUIRE DAYTIMES, SUITE 1, MAISON FEMA

"You'd think I'd be tired of this by now," Darger commented during a brief break in the ritual. "And yet I am not."

"The infinite variety of ways in which women can be beautiful is indeed amazing," Surplus agreed. "As is the eagerness of so many to display that beauty." He opened the door. "Next."

A woman strode into the room, trailing smoke from a cheroot. She was dauntingly tall—six feet and a hand, if an inch—and her dress, trimmed with silver lace, was the same shade of golden brown as her skin. Surplus indicated a crystal ashtray on the sideboard and, with a gracious nod of thanks, she stubbed out her cigar.

"Your name?" Darger said after Surplus had regained his chair.

"My real name, you mean, or my stage name?"

"Why, whichever you please."

"I'll give you the real one then." The young woman doffed her hat and tugged off her gloves. She laid them neatly together on the sideboard. "It's Tawnymoor Petticoats. You can call me Tawny."

"Tell us something about yourself, Tawny," Surplus said.

"I was born a carny and worked forty-milers all my life," Tawny said, unbuttoning her blouse. "Most recently, I was in the sideshow as the Sleeping Beauty Made Immortal by Utopian Technology But Doomed Never to Awaken. I lay in a glass coffin covered by nothing but my own hair and a strategically placed hand, while the audience tried to figure out if I was alive or not. I've got good breath control." She folded the blouse and set it down by her gloves and hat. "Jake—my husband—was the barker. He'd size up the audience and when he saw a ripe mark, catch 'im on the way out and whisper that for a couple of banknotes it could be arranged to spend some private time with me. Then he'd go out back and peer in through a slit in the canvas."

Tawny stepped out of her skirt and set it atop the blouse. She began unlacing her petticoats. "When the mark had his trousers off and was about to climb in the coffin, Jake would come roaring out, bellowing that he was only supposed to look—not to take advantage of my vulnerable condition." Placing her underthings atop the skirt, she undid her garters and proceeded to roll down her stockings. "That was usually good for the contents of his wallet."

"You were working the badger game, you mean?" Surplus asked cautiously.

"Mostly, I just lay there. But I was ready to rear up and cold-cock the sumbidge if he got out of hand. And we worked other scams too. The pigeon drop, the fiddle game, the rip deal, you name it."

Totally naked now, the young woman lifted her great masses of black curls with both hands, exposing the back of her neck. "Then one night the mark was halfway into the coffin—and no Jake. So I opened my eyes real sudden and screamed in the bastard's face. Over he went, hit his head on the floor, and I didn't wait to find out if he was unconscious or dead. I stole his jacket and went looking for my husband. Turns out Jake had run off with the Snake Woman. She dumped him two weeks later and he wanted me to take him back, but I wasn't having none of that." She turned around slowly, so that Darger and Surplus could examine every inch of her undeniably admirable flesh.

Darger cleared his throat. "Um…you don't appear to have a tattoo."

"Yeah, I saw through that one right away. Talked to some of the girls you'd interviewed and they said you'd asked them lots of questions about themselves but hadn't molested them in any way. Not all of 'em were happy with that last bit. Particularly after they'd gone to all the trouble of getting themselves inked. So, putting two and four together, I figured you were running a scam requiring a female partner with quick wits and larcenous proclivities."

Tawny Petticoats put her hands on her hips and smiled. "Well? Do I get the job?"

Grinning like a dog—which was not surprising, for his source genome was entirely canine— Surplus stood, extending a paw. But Darger quickly got between him and the young woman, saying, "If you will pardon us for just a moment, Ms. Petticoats, my friend and I must consult in the back room. You may use the time to dress yourself."

When the two males were secluded, Darger whispered furiously, "Thank God I was able to stop you! You were about to enlist that young woman into our conspiracy."

"Well, and why not?" Surplus murmured equally quietly. "We were looking for a woman of striking appearance, not overly bound to conventional morality, and possessed of the self-confidence, initiative, and inventiveness a good swindler requires. Tawny comes up aces on all counts."

"Working with an amateur is one thing—but this woman is a professional. She will sleep with both of us, turn us against each other, and in the end abscond with the swag, leaving us with nothing but embarrassment and regret for all our efforts."

"That is a sexist and, if I may dare say so, ungallant slander upon the fair sex, and I am astonished to hear it coming from your mouth."

Darger shook his head sadly. "It is not all women but all female confidence tricksters I abjure. I speak from sad—and repeated—experience."

"Well, if you insist on doing without this blameless young creature," Surplus said, folding his arms, "then I insist on your doing without me."

"My dear sir!"

"I must be true to my principles."

Further argumentation, Darger saw, would be useless. So, putting the best possible appearance on things, he emerged from the back room to say, "You have the job, my dear." From a jacket pocket he produced a silver filigreed vinaigrette and, unscrewing its cap, extracted from it a single pill. "Swallow this and you'll have the tattoo we require by morning. You'll want to run it past your pharmacist first, of course, to verify—"

"Oh, I trust you. If y'all had just been after tail, you wouldn't've waited for me. Some of those gals was sharp lookers for sure." Tawny swallowed the pill. "So what's the dodge?"

"We're going to work the black money scam," Surplus said.

"Oh, I have always wanted a shot at running that one!" With a whoop, Tawny threw her arms about them both.

Though his fingers itched to do so, Darger was very careful not to check to see if his wallet was still there.

\෪

THE NEXT DAY, ten crates of black money—actually, rectangles of scrap parchment dyed black in distant Vicksburg—were carried into the hotel by zombie laborers and then, at Surplus's direction, piled against the outside of Tawny's door so that, hers being the central room of the suite, the only way to enter or leave it was through his or Darger's rooms. Then, leaving the lady to see to her dress and makeup, her new partners set out to speak to their respective marks.

Darger began at the city's busy docklands.

The office of the speculator Jean-Nagin Lafitte was tastefully opulent and dominated by a Mauisaurus skull, decorated with scrimshaw filigree chased in silver. "Duke" Lafitte, as he styled himself, or "Pirate" Lafitte, as he was universally known, was a slim, handsome man with olive skin, long and flowing hair, and a mustache so thin it might have been drawn on with an eyebrow pencil. Where other men of wealth might carry a cane, he affected a coiled whip, which he wore on his belt.

"Renting an ingot of silver!" he exclaimed. "I never heard of such a thing."

"It is a simple enough proposition," Darger said. "Silver serves as a catalyst for a certain bioindustrial process, the precise nature of which I am not at liberty to divulge to you. The scheme involves converting bar silver to a colloidal slurry which, when the process is complete, will be recovered and melted back into bar form. You would lose nothing. Further, we will only tie up your wealth for, oh, let us say ten days to be on the safe side. In return for which we are prepared to offer you a ten percent return on your investment. A very tidy profit for no risk at all."

A small and ruthless smile played upon the speculator's lips. "There is the risk of your simply taking the silver and absconding with it."

"That is an outrageous implication, and from a man I respected less highly than I do you, I would not put up with it. However"—Darger gestured out the window at the busy warehouses and transshipment buildings—"I understand that you own half of everything we see. Lend my consortium a building in which to perform our operation and then place as many guards as you like around that building. We will bring in our apparatus and you will bring in the silver. Deal?"

For a brief moment, Pirate Lafitte hesitated. Then, "Done!" he snapped, and offered his hand. "For fifteen percent. Plus rental of the building."

They shook, and Darger said, "You will have no objection to having the ingot tested by a reputable assayist."

IN THE FRENCH Quarter, meanwhile, Surplus was having an almost identical conversation with a slight and acerbic woman, clad in a severe black dress, who was not only the mayor of New Orleans but also the proprietress of its largest and most notorious brothel. Behind her, alert and unspeaking, stood two uniformed ape-men from the Canadian Northwest, both with the expressions of baffled anger common to beasts that have been elevated almost but not quite to human intelligence. "An assayist?" she demanded. "Is my word not good enough for you? And if it is not, should we be doing business at all?"

"The answer to all three of your questions, Madam-Mayor Tresjolie, is yes," Surplus said amiably. "The assay is for your own protection. As you doubtless know, silver is routinely adulterated with other metals. When we are done with the silver, the slurry will be melted down and recast into an ingot. Certainly, you will want to know that the bar returned to you is of equal worth to the bar you rented out."

"Hmmm." They were sitting in the lobby of the madam-mayor's maison de tolérance, she in a flaring wicker chair whose similarity to a throne could not possibly be unintentional, and Surplus on a wooden folding chair facing her. Because it was still early afternoon, the facility was not open for business. But messengers and government flunkies came and went. Now one such whispered in

Madam-Mayor Tresjolie's ear. She waved him away. "Seventeen and a half percent, take it or leave it."

"I'll take it."

"Good," Tresjolie said. "I have business with the zombie master now. Move your chair alongside mine, and stay to watch. If we are to do business, you will find this salubrious."

A round and cheerful man entered the public room, followed by half a dozen zombies. Surplus studied these with interest. Though their eyes were dull, their faces were stiff, and there was an unhealthy sheen to their skin, they looked in no way like the rotting corpses of Utopian legend. Rather, they looked like day laborers who had been worked into a state of complete exhaustion. Which doubtless was the case.

"Good morning!" said the jolly man, rubbing his hands briskly together. "I have brought this week's coffle of debtors who, having served their time, are now eligible for forgiveness and manumission."

"I had wondered at the source of your involuntary labor force," Surplus said. "They are unfortunates who fell into arrears, then?"

"Exactly so," said the zombie master. "New Orleans does not engage in the barbarous and expensive practice of funding debtors' prisons. Instead, debt-criminals are chemically rendered incapable of independent thought and put to work until they have paid off their debt to society. Which today's happy fellows have done." With a roguish wink, he added, "You may want to keep this in mind before running up too great a line of credit at the rooms upstairs. Are you ready to begin, Madam-Mayor Tresjolie?"

"You may proceed, Master Bones."

Master Bones gestured imperiously and the first zombie shuffled forward. "Through profligacy you fell into debt," he said, "and through honest labor you have earned your way out. Open your mouth."

The pallid creature obeyed. Master Bones produced a spoon and dipped into a salt cellar on a nearby table. He dumped the salt into the man's mouth. "Now swallow."

By gradual degrees, a remarkable transformation came over the man. He straightened and looked about him with tentative alertness. "I…" he said. "I remember now. Is my…is my wife…?"

"Silence," the zombie master said. "The ceremony is not yet complete." The Canadian guardsmen had shifted position to defend their mistress, should the disoriented ex-zombie attack her.

"You are hereby declared a free citizen of New Orleans again, and indebted to no man," Tresjolie said solemnly. "Go and over-spend no more." She extended a leg and lifted her skirts above her ankle. "You may now kiss my foot."

\ঙৎৗৎ/

"SO DID YOU ask Tresjolie for a line of credit at her sporting house?" Tawny asked when Surplus reported his adventure to his confederates.

"Certainly not!" Surplus exclaimed. "I told her instead that it has always been my ambition to own a small but select private brothel, one dedicated solely to my own personal use. A harem, if you will, but one peopled by a rotating staff of well-paid employ-ees. I suggested I might shortly be in a position to commission her to find an appropriate hotel and create such an institution for me."

"What did she say?"

"She told me that she doubted I was aware of exactly how expensive such an operation would be."

"And you said to her?

"That I didn't think money would be problem," Surplus said airily. "Because I expected to come into a great deal of it very soon."

Tawny crowed with delight. "Oh, you boys are such fun!"

"In unrelated news," Darger said, "your new dress has come."

"I saw it when it first arrived." Tawny made a face. "It is not calculated to show off my body to its best advantage—or to any advantage at all, come to that."

"It is indeed aggressively modest," Darger agreed. "However, your character is demure and inexperienced. To her innocent eyes, New Orleans is a terribly wicked place, indeed a cesspool of carnality and related sins. Therefore, she needs to be protected at all times by unrevealing apparel and stalwart men of the highest moral character."

"Further," Surplus amplified, "she is the weak point in our plans, for whoever has possession of her tattoo and knows its meaning can dispense with us entirely by kidnapping her off the street."

"Oh!" Tawny said in a small voice, clearly intended to arouse the protective instincts of any man nearby.

Surplus took an instinctive step toward her, and then caught himself. He grinned like the carnivore he was. "You'll do."

♥

THE THIRD MEETING with a potential investor took place that evening in a dimly lit club in a rundown parish on the fringe of the French Quarter—for the entertainment was, in the public mind, far too louche for even that notoriously open-minded neighborhood. Pallid waitresses moved lifelessly between the small tables, taking orders and delivering drinks while a small brass-and-drums jazz ensemble played appropriately sleazy music to accompany the stage show.

"I see that you are no aficionado of live sex displays," the zombie master Jeremy Bones said. The light from the candle votive on the table made the beads of sweat on his face shine like luminous drops of rain.

"The artistic success of such displays depends entirely on the degree to which they agree with one's own sexual proclivities," Darger replied. "I confess that mine lie elsewhere. But never mind that. Returning to the subject at hand: The terms are agreeable to you, then?"

"They are. I am unclear, however, as to why you insist the assay be performed at the Bank of San Francisco, when New Orleans has several fine financial institutions of its own."

"All of which are owned in part by you, Madam-Mayor Tresjolie, and Duke Lafitte."

"Pirate Lafitte, you mean. An assay is an assay and a bank is a bank. Why should it matter to you which one is employed?"

"Earlier today, you brought six zombies to the mayor to be freed. Assuming this is a typical week, that would be roughly three hundred zombies per year. Yet all the menial work in the city has been handed over to zombies and there still remain tens of thousands at work in the plantations that line the river."

"Many of those who fall into debt draw multi-year sentences."

"I asked around, and discovered that Lafitte's ships import some two hundred prisoners a week from municipalities and territories all the way up the Mississippi to St. Louis."

A small smile played on the fat man's face. "It is true that many government bodies find it cheaper to pay us to deal with their troublemakers than to build prisons for them."

"Madam-Mayor Tresjolie condemns these unfortunates into the city's penal system, you pay her by body count, and after they have been zombified you lease them out for menial labor at prices that employers find irresistible. Those who enter your service rarely leave it."

"If a government official or family member presents me with papers proving that somebody's debt to society has been paid off, I am invariably happy to free them. I grant you that few ever come to me with such documentation. But I am always available to those who do. Exactly what is your objection to this arrangement?"

"Objection?" Darger said in surprise. "I have no objection. This is your system and as an outsider I have no say in it. I am merely explaining the reason why I wished to use an independent bank for the assay."

"Which is?"

"Simply that, happy though I am to deal with you three individually, collectively I find you far too shrewd." Darger turned to stare at the stage, where naked zombies coupled joylessly. Near the front, a spectator removed several banknotes from his wallet and tapped them meaningfully on his table. One of the lifeless waitresses picked up the money and led him through a curtain at the back of the room. "Acting together, I suspect you would swallow me and my partners in a single gulp."

"Oh, there is no fear of that," Master Bones said. "We three only act collectively when there is serious profit in the offing. Your little enterprise—whatever it is—hardly qualifies."

"I am relieved to hear it."

♮

THE NEXT DAY, the three conspirators made three distinct trips to the Assay Office at the New Orleans branch of the Bank of San Francisco. On the first trip, one of Madam-Mayor Tresjolie's green-jacketed zombie bodyguards opened a lockbox, withdrew a silver ingot, and placed it on the workbench. Then, to the astonishment of both the mayor and the assayist, Surplus directed his own hired zombies to hoist several heavy leather bags to the bench as well, and with the aid of his colleagues began pulling out drills, scales, acids, reagents, and other tools and supplies and setting them in working order.

The affronted assayist opened his mouth to object, but—"I'm sure you won't mind if we provide our own equipment," Darger said suavely. "We are strangers here, and while nobody questions the probity of San Francisco's most prestigious financial concern, it is only good business to take proper precautions."

As he was talking, Tawny and Surplus both reached for the scales at once, collided, and almost sent them flying. Faces turned and hands reached out to catch them. But, in the fact, it was Surplus who saved the apparatus from disaster.

"Oops," Tawny said, coloring prettily.

Swiftly, the assayist performed his tests. At their conclusion, he looked up from the ingot. "The finding is .925," he said. "Sterling standard."

With an absent nod, Madam-Mayor Tresjolie acknowledged his judgment. Then she said, "The girl. How much do you want for her?"

As one, Darger and Surplus turned. Then they subtly shifted position so that one stood to either side of Tawny. "Ms. Petticoats is our ward," Darger said, "and therefore, it goes without saying, not for sale. Also, yours is not an entirely reputable business for so innocent a child as she."

"Innocence is in high demand at my establishment. I'll give you the silver ingot. To keep. Do with it as you wish."

"Believe me, madam. In not so very long, I shall consider silver ingots to be so much petty cash."

MASTER BONES WATCHED the assay, including even the chaotic assembly of the trio's equipment, with a beatific smile. Yet all the while, his attention kept straying to Tawny. Finally, he pursed his lips and said, "There might be a place in my club for your young friend. If you'd consider leasing her to me for, oh, let's say a year, I'd gladly forego my twenty percent profit on this deal." Turning to Tawny, he said, "Do not worry, my sweet. Under the influence of the zombie drugs you will feel nothing, and afterwards you will remember nothing. It will be as if none of it ever happened. Further, since you'd be paid a commission on each commercial encounter performed, you'd emerge with a respectable sum being held in trust for you."

Ignoring Tawny's glare of outrage, Darger suavely said, "In strictest confidence, sir, we have already turned down a far better offer for her than yours today. But my partner and I would not part with our dear companion for any amount of money. She is to us a treasure beyond price."

"I'm ready," the assayist said. "Where do you wish me to drill?"

Darger airily waved a finger over the ingot and then, seemingly at random, touched a spot at the exact center of the bar. "Right there."

"I UNDERSTAND THAT on the street they call me the Pirate," Jean-Nagin Lafitte said with quiet intensity. "This, however, is an insolence I will not tolerate to my face. Yes, I do chance to share a name with the legendary freebooter. But you will find that I have never committed an illegal act in my life."

"Nor do you today, sir!" Darger cried. "This is a strictly legitimate business arrangement."

"So I presume or I would not be here. Nevertheless, you can understand why I must take offense at having you and your clumsy confederates question the quality of my silver."

"Say no more, sir! We are all gentlemen here—save, of course, for Ms. Petticoats who is a gently-reared Christian orphan. If my word is good enough for you, then your word is good enough for me. We may dispose of the assay." Darger coughed discreetly. "However, just for my own legal protection, in the absence of an assay, I shall require a notarized statement from you declaring that you will be satisfied with whatever quality of silver we return to you."

Pirate Lafitte's stare would have melted iron. But it failed to wilt Darger's pleasant smile. At last, he said, "Very well, run the assay."

Negligently, Darger spun a finger in the air. Down it came on the exact center of the bar. "There."

While the assayist was working, Pirate Lafitte said, "I was wondering if your Miss Petticoats might be available to—"

"She is not for sale!" Darger said briskly. "Not for sale, not for rent, not for barter, not available for acquisition on any terms whatsoever. Period."

Looking irritated, Pirate Lafitte said, "I was going to ask if she might be interested in going hunting with me tomorrow. There is some interesting game to be found in the bayous."

"Nor is she available for social occasions." Darger turned to the assayist. "Well, sir?"

"Standard sterling," the man said. "Yet again."

"I expected no less."

FOR THE SAKE of appearances, after the assays were complete, the three swindlers sent the zombies with their lab equipment back to Mason Fema and went out to supper together. Following which, they took a genteel stroll about town. Tawny, who had been confined to her room while negotiations took place, was particularly glad of the latter. But it was with relief that Darger, Surplus, and Tawny saw the heavy bags waiting for them on the sitting room table of their suite. "Who shall do the honors?" Darger asked.

"The lady, of course," Surplus said with a little bow.

Tawny curtsied and then, pushing aside a hidden latch at the bottom of one of the bags, slid out a silver ingot. From another bag, she slid out a second. Then, from a third, a third. A sigh of relief went up from all three conspirators at the sight of the silver glimmering in the lantern-light.

"That was right smartly done, when you changed the fake bars for the real ones," Tawny said.

Darger politely demurred. "No, it was the distraction that made the trick possible, and in this regard you were both exemplary. Even the assayist, who was present all three times you almost sent the equipment to the floor, suspected nothing."

"But tell me something," Tawny said. "Why did you make the substitution before the assay, rather than after? The other way around, you wouldn't have needed to have that little plug of silver in the middle for the sample to be drawn from. Just a silver-plated lead bar."

"We are dealing with suspicious people. This way, they first had the ingots confirmed as genuine and then saw that we came nowhere near them afterwards. The ingots are in a safety deposit box in a reputable bank, so to their minds there is not the least risk. All is on the up-and-up."

"But we're not going to stop here, are we?" Tawny asked anxiously. "I do so want to work the black money scam."

"Have no fear, my lovely," Surplus said, "this is only the beginning. But it serves as a kind of insurance policy for us. Even should the scheme go bad, we have already turned a solid profit." He poured brandy into three small glasses and handed them around. "To whom shall we drink?"

"To Madam-Mayor Tresjolie!" Darger said.

They drank, and then Tawny said, "What do you make of her? Professionally, I mean."

"She is far shrewder than she would have you think," Surplus replied. "But, as you are doubtless aware, the self-consciously shrewd are always the easiest to mislead." He poured a second glass. "To Master Bones!"

They drank. Tawny said, "And of him?"

"He is more problematic," Darger said. "A soft man with a brutal streak underneath his softness. In some ways he hardly seems human."

"Perhaps he has been sampling his own product?" Surplus suggested.

"Puffer fish extract, you mean? No. His mind is active enough. But I catch not the least glimmer of empathy from him. I suspect that he's been associating with zombies so long that he's come to think we're all like them."

The final toast inevitably went to Pirate Lafitte.

"I think he's cute," Tawny said. "Only maybe you don't agree?"

"He is a fraud and a poseur," Darger replied, "a scoundrel who passes himself off as a gentleman, and a manipulator of the legal system who insists he is the most honest of citizens. Consequently, I like him quite a bit. I believe that he is a man we can do business with. Mark my words, when the three of them come to see us tomorrow, it will be at his instigation."

For a time they talked business. Then Surplus broke out a deck of cards. They played euchre and canasta and poker, and because they played for matches, nobody objected when the game turned into a competition to see how deftly the cards could be dealt from the bottom of the deck or flicked out of the sleeve into one's hand. Nor was there any particular outcry when in one memorable hand, eleven aces were laid on the table at once.

At last Darger said, "Look at the time! It will be a long day tomorrow," and they each went to their respective rooms.

THAT NIGHT, AS Darger was drifting off to sleep, he heard the door connecting his room with Tawny's quietly open and shut. There was a rustle of sheets as she slipped into his bed. Then the warmth of Tawny's naked body pressed against his own, and her hand closed about his most private part. Abruptly, he was wide awake.

"What on earth do you think you're doing?" he whispered fiercely.

Unexpectedly, Tawny released her hold on Darger and punched him hard in his shoulder. "Oh, it's so easy for you," she retorted, equally quietly. "It's so easy for men! That hideous old woman tried to buy me. That awful little man wanted you to let him drug me. And God only knows what intentions Pirate Lafitte holds. You'll notice they all made their propositions to you. Not a one of them said a word to me." Hot tears fell on Darger's chest. "All my life I have had male protectors—and needed them too. My Daddy, until I ran away. My first husband, until he got eaten by giant crabs. Then various boyfriends and finally that creep Jake."

"You have nothing to worry about. Surplus and I have never abandoned a confederate, nor shall we ever. Our reputation is spotless in this regard."

"I tell myself that, and daytimes I'm fine with it. But at night… well, this past week has been the longest I ever went without a man's body to comfort me."

"Yes, but surely you understand—"

Tawny drew herself up. Even in the dim half light of the moon through the window she was a magnificent sight. Then she leaned down to kiss Darger's cheek and murmured into his ear, "I've never had to beg a man before, but... Please?"

Darger considered himself a moral man. But there was only so much temptation a man could resist without losing all respect for himself.

THE NEXT MORNING, Darger awoke alone. He thought of the events of last night and smiled. He thought of their implications and scowled. Then he went down to the dining room for breakfast.

"What comes next?" Tawny asked, after they had fortified themselves with chicory coffee, beignets, and sliced baconfruit.

"We have planted suspicions in the minds of our three backers that there is more profit to be had than we are offering to share," Surplus said. "We have given them a glimpse of our mysterious young ward and suggested that she is key to the enterprise. We have presented them with a puzzle to which they can think of no solution. On reflection, they can only conclude that the sole reason we have the upper hand is that we can play them off of one another." He popped the last of his beignet into his mouth. "So sooner or later they will unite and demand of us an explanation."

"In the meantime—" Darger said.

"I know, I know. Back to my dreary old room to play solitaire and read the sort of uplifting literature appropriate to a modest young virgin."

"It's important to stay in character," Surplus said.

"I understand that. Next time, however, please make me something that doesn't need to be stored in the dark, like a sack of potatoes. The niece of a Spanish prisoner, perhaps. Or a socialite heiress. Or even a harlot."

"You are a Woman of Mystery," Darger said. "Which is a time-honored and some would say enviable role to play."

Thus it was that when Darger and Surplus left Maison Fema—at precisely ten o'clock, as they had made it their invariant habit—they were not entirely astonished to find their three benefactors all in a group, waiting for them. A brusque exchange of threats and outrage later, and protesting every step of the way, they led their marks to their suite.

The three bedrooms all opened off of a sunny common room. Given the room's elegant appointments, the crates of black paper that had been stacked in front of Tawny Petticoats' door looked glaringly out of place.

Gesturing their guests to chairs, Darger adopted an air of resignation and said, "In order to adequately explain our enterprise, we must go back two generations to a time before San Francisco became the financial center of North America. The visionary leaders of that great city-state determined to found a new economy upon uncounterfeitable banknotes, and to this end employed the greatest bacterial engraver of his age, Phineas Whipsnade McGonigle."

"That is an unlikely name," Madam-Mayor Tresjolie sniffed.

"It was of course his nom de gravure, assumed to protect him from kidnappers and the like," Surplus explained. "In private life, he was known as Magnus Norton."

"Go on."

Darger resumed his narrative. "The results you know. Norton crafted one hundred and thirteen different bacteria which, as part of their natural functions, laid down layer upon layer of multicolored ink in delicate arabesques so intricate as to be the despair of coin-clippers and paperhangers everywhere. This, combined with their impeccable monetary policies, has made the San Francisco dollar the common currency of the hundred nations of North America. Alas for them, there was one weak point in their enterprise—Norton himself.

"Norton secretly created his own printing vats, employing the bacteria he himself had created, and proceeded to mass-produce banknotes that were not only indistinguishable from the genuine item but for all intents and purposes were the genuine item. He created enough of them to make himself the wealthiest man on the continent.

"Unfortunately for that great man, he tried to underpay his paper supplier, precipitating an argument that ended with him being arrested by the San Francisco authorities."

Pirate Lafitte raised an elegant forefinger. "How do you know all this?" he asked.

"My colleague and I are journalists," Darger said. Seeing his audience's expressions, he raised both hands. "Not of the muckraking variety, I hasten to assure you! Corruption is a necessary and time-honored concomitant of any functioning government, and one we support wholeheartedly. No, we write profiles of public figures, lavishing praise in direct proportion to their private generosity; human interest stories of heroic boys rescuing heiresses from fires and of kittens swallowed by crocodiles and yet miraculously passing through their alimentary systems unharmed; and of course amusing looks back at the forgotten histories of local scoundrels whom the passage of time has rendered unthreatening."

"It was this last that led us to Norton's story," Surplus elucidated.

"Indeed. We discovered that by a quirk of San Francisco's labyrinthine banking regulations, Norton's monetary creations could neither be destroyed nor distributed as valid currency. So to prevent their misuse, the banknotes were subjected to another bio-lithographic process whereby they were deeply impregnated with black ink so cunningly composed that no known process could bleach it from the bills without destroying the paper in the process.

"Now, here's where our tale gets interesting. Norton was, you'll recall, incomparable in his craft. Naturally, the city fathers were reluctant to forgo his services. So, rather than have him languish in an ordinary prison, they walled and fortified a mansion, equipped it with a laboratory and all the resources he required, and put him to work.

"Imagine how Norton felt! One moment he was on the brink of realizing vast wealth, and the next he was a virtual slave. So long as he cooperated, he was given fine foods, wine, even conjugal visits with his wife… But, comfortable though his prison was, he could never leave it. He was, however, a cunning man and though he could not engineer his escape, he managed to devise a means of revenge: If he could not have vast wealth, then his descendants would. Someday, the provenance of the black paper would be forgotten and it would be put up for public auction as eventually occurs to all the useless lumber a bureaucracy acquires. His children or grandchildren or great-great-grandchildren would acquire it and, utilizing an ingenious method of his own devising, convert it back into working currency and so make themselves rich beyond Croesus."

"The ancients had a saying," Surplus interjected. "'If you want to make God laugh, tell him your plans.' The decades passed, Norton died, and the black paper stayed in storage. By the time we began our researches, his family was apparently extinct. He had three children: a daughter who was not interested in men, a son who died young, and another son who never wed. The second son, however, traveled about in his early adulthood, and in the same neglected cache of family papers where we discovered Norton's plans, we found evidence that he was paying child support for a female bastard he had sired here some twenty years ago. So, utilizing an understanding of the city bureaucracy which Norton's wife and children lacked, we bribed the appropriate official to sell us the crates of seemingly worthless paper and came to New Orleans. Where we found Tawny Petticoats."

"This explains nothing," Madam-Mayor Tresjolie said.

Darger sighed heavily. "We had hoped you would be satisfied with a partial explanation. Now I see that it is all or nothing. Here before you are the crates of blackened banknotes." A plank had been removed from one of the topmost crates. He reached in to seize a handful of black paper rectangles, fanned them for all to see, and then put them back. "My colleague and I will now introduce you to our young charge."

Swiftly, Darger and Surplus unstacked the crates before the doorway, placing them to either side. Then Surplus rapped on the door. "Ms. Petticoats? Are you decent? We have visitors to see you."

The door opened. Tawny's large brown eyes peered apprehensively from the gloom. "Come in," she said in a little voice.

They all shuffled inside. Tawny looked first at Darger and then at Surplus. When they would not meet her eyes, she ducked her head, blushing. "I guess I know what y'all came here to see. Only... must I? Must I really?"

"Yes, child, you must," Surplus said gruffly.

Tawny tightened her mouth and raised her chin, staring straight ahead of herself like the captain of a schooner sailing into treacherous waters. Reaching around her back, she began unbuttoning her dress.

"Magnus Norton designed what no other man could have—a microorganism that would eat the black ink permeating the banknotes without damaging the other inks in any way. Simply place the notes in the proper liquid nutrient, add powdered silver as a catalyst, and within a week there will be nothing but perfect San Francisco money and a slurry of silver," Darger said. "However, he still faced the problem of passing the information of how to create the organism to his family. In a manner, moreover, robust enough to survive what he knew would be decades of neglect."

Tawny had unbuttoned her dress. Now, placing a hand upon her bosom to hold the dress in place, she drew one arm from its sleeve. Then, switching hands, she drew out the other. "Now?" she said.

Surplus nodded.

With tiny, doll-like steps, Tawny turned to face the wall. Then she lowered her dress so that they could see her naked back. On it was a large tattoo in seven bright colors, of three concentric circles. Each circle was made of a great number of short, near-parallel lines, all radiant from the unmarked skin at the tattoo's center. Anyone who could read a gene map could easily use it to create the organism it described.

Master Bones, who had not spoken before now, said, "That's an E. coli, isn't it?"

"A variant on it, yes, sir. Norton wrote this tattoo into his own genome and then sired three children upon his wife, believing they would have many more in their turn. But fate is a fickle lady, and Ms. Petticoats is the last of her line. She, however, will suffice." He turned to Tawny. "You may clothe yourself again. Our guests have had their curiosities satisfied, and now they will leave."

Darger led the group back to the front room, closing the door firmly behind him. "Now," he said. "You have learned what you came to learn. At the cost, I might mention, of violently depriving an innocent maiden of her modesty."

"That is a swinish thing to say!" Pirate Lafitte snapped.

In the silence that followed his outburst, all could hear Tawny Petticoats in the next room, sobbing her heart out.

"Your work here is done," Darger said, "and I must ask you to leave."

NOW THAT TAWNY Petticoats was no longer a secret, there was nothing for the three conspirators to do but wait for the equipment they had supposedly sent for upriver—and for their marks to each separately approach them with very large bribes to buy their process and the crates of black paper away from them. As simple logic stipulated that they inevitably must.

The very next day, after the morning mail had brought two notes proposing meetings, the trio went out for breakfast at a side-walk café. They had just finished and were beginning their second cups of coffee when Tawny looked over Darger's shoulder and exclaimed, "Oh, merciful God in heaven! It's Jake." Then, seeing her companions' incomprehension, "My husband! He's talking to Pirate Lafitte. They're coming this way."

"Keep smiling," Darger murmured. "Feign unconcern. Surplus, you know what to do."

It took a count of ten for the interlopers to reach their table.

"Jake!" Surplus exclaimed in evident surprise, beginning to rise from his chair.

"Come for his pay, no doubt." Darger drew from his pocket the wad of bills—one of large denomination on the outside, a great many singles beneath—which any sensible businessman carried with him at all times and, turning, said, "The madam-mayor wishes you to know—"

He found himself confronted by a stranger who could only be Tawny's Jake and Pirate Lafitte, whose face was contorted with astonishment.

Darger hastily thrust the wad of bills back into his pocket. "Wishes you to know," he repeated, "that, ah, anytime you wish to try out her establishment, she will gladly offer you a ten percent discount on all goods and services, alcohol excepted. It is a courtesy she has newly decided to extend, out of respect for your employer, to all his new hires."

Lafitte turned, grabbed Jake by the shirtfront, and shook him as a mastiff might a rat. "I understand now," he said through gritted teeth. "The honorable brothel-keeper wished to deal me out of a rich opportunity, and so she sent you to me with a cock-and-bull story about this virtuous and inoffensive young woman."

"Honest, boss, I ain't got the slightest idea what this...this... foreigner is talking about. It's honest info I'm peddling here. I heard it on the street that my filthy bitch of a—"

With a roar of rage, Pirate Lafitte punched Jake so hard he fell sprawling in the street. Then he pulled the whip from his belt and proceeded to lay into the man so savagely that by the time he was done, his shirt and vest were damp with sweat.

Breathing heavily from exertion, he touched his hat to Darger and Surplus. "Sirs. We shall talk later, at a time when my passions are not so excited. This afternoon, five o'clock, at my office. I have a proposition to put to you." Then, to Tawny, "Miss Petticoats, I apologize that you had to see this."

He strode off.

"Oh!" Tawny breathed. "He beat Jake within an inch of his worthless life. It was the most romantic thing I ever seen in my life."

"A horsewhipping? Romantic?" Darger said.

Tawny favored him with a superior look. "You don't much understand the workings of a woman's heart, do you?"

"Apparently not," Darger said. "And it begins to appear that I never shall." Out in the street, Jake was painfully pulling himself up and trying to stand. "Excuse me."

Darger went over to the battered and bleeding man and helped him to his feet. Then, talking quietly, he opened his billfold and thrust several notes into the man's hand.

"What did you give him?" Tawny asked, when he was back inside.

"A stern warning not to interfere with us again. Also, seventeen dollars. A sum insulting enough to guarantee that, despite his injuries, he will take his increasingly implausible story to Master Bones, and then to the Madam-Mayor."

Tawny grabbed Darger and Surplus and hugged them both at once. "Oh, you boys are so good to me. I just love you both to pieces and back."

"It begins to look, however," Surplus said. "Like we have been stood up. According to Madam-Mayor Tresjolie's note, she should have been here by now. Which is, if I may use such language, damnably peculiar."

"Something must have come up." Darger squinted up at the sky. "Tresjolie isn't here and it's about time for the meeting with Master Bones. You should stay here, in case the madam-mayor shows up. I'll see what the zombie master has to say."

"And I," Tawny said, "will go back to my room to adjust my dress."

"Adjust?" Surplus asked.

"It needs to be a little tighter and to show just a smidge more bosom."

Alarmed, Darger said, "Your character is a modest and innocent thing."

"She is a modest and innocent thing who secretly wishes a worldly cad would teach her all those wicked deeds she has heard about but cannot quite imagine. I have played this role before, gentlemen. Trust me, it is not innocence per se that men like Pirate Lafitte are drawn to but the tantalizing possibility of corrupting that innocence."

Then she was gone.

"A most remarkable young lady, our Ms. Petticoats," Surplus said.

Darger scowled.

AFTER DARGER LEFT, Surplus leaned back in his chair for some casual people watching. He had not been at it long when he noticed that a remarkably pretty woman at a table at the far end of the café kept glancing his way. When he returned her gaze, she blushed and looked quickly away.

From long experience, Surplus understood what such looks meant. Leaving money on the table to pay for the breakfasts, he strolled over to introduce himself to the lady. She seemed not unreceptive to his attentions, and after a remarkably short conversation, invited him to her room in a nearby hotel. Feigning surprise, Surplus accepted.

What happened there had occurred many times before in his eventful life. But that didn't make it any less delightful.

On leaving the hotel, however, Surplus was alarmed to find himself abruptly seized and firmly held by two red-furred, seven-foot-tall uniformed Canadian ape-men.

"I see you have been entertaining yourself with one of the local sluts," Madam-Mayor Tresjolie said. She looked even less benevolent than usual.

"That is a harsh characterization of a lady who, for all I know, may be of high moral character. Also, I must ask you why I am being held captive like this."

"In due time. First, tell me whether your encounter was a commercial one or not."

"I thought not when we were in the throes of it. But afterward, she showed me her union card and informed me that as a matter of policy she was required to charge not only by the hour but by the position. I was, of course, astonished."

"What did you do then?"

"I paid, of course," Surplus said indignantly. "I am no scab!"

"The woman with whom you coupled, however, was not a registered member of the International Sisterhood of Trollops, Demimondaines, and Back-Alley Doxies and her card was a forgery. Which means that while nobody objects to your non-commercial sexual activities, by paying her you were engaged in a union-busting activity—and that, sir, is against the law."

"Obviously, you set me up. Otherwise, you could have known none of this."

"That is neither here nor there. What is relevant is that you have three things that I want—the girl with the birthmark, the crates of money, and the knowledge of how to use the one to render the other negotiable."

"I understand now. Doubtless, madam, you seek to bribe me. I assure you that no amount of money—"

"Money?" The madam-mayor's laugh was short and harsh. "I am offering you something far more precious: your conscious mind." She produced a hypodermic needle. "People think the zombification formula consists entirely of extract of puffer fish. But in fact atropine, datura, and a dozen other drugs are involved, all blended in a manner guaranteed to make the experience very unpleasant indeed."

"Threats will not work on me."

"Not yet. But after you've had a taste of what otherwise lies before you, I'm sure you'll come around. In a week or so, I'll haul you back from the fields. Then we can negotiate."

Madam-Mayor Tresjolie's simian thugs held Surplus firmly, struggle though he did. She raised the syringe to his neck. There was a sharp sting.

The world went away.

ୖ୧ଢ଼

DARGER, MEANWHILE, HAD rented a megatherium, complete with howdah and zombie mahout, and ridden it to the endless rows of zombie barns, pens, and feeding sheds at the edge of town. There, Master Bones showed him the chest-high troughs that were filled with swill every morning and evening, and the rows of tin spoons the sad creatures used to feed themselves. "When each of my pretties has fed, the spoon is set aside to be washed and sterilized before it is used again," Master Bones said. "Every precaution is taken to ensure they do not pass diseases from one to another."

"Commendably humane, sir. To say nothing of it being good business practice."

"You understand me well." They passed outside, where a pair of zombies, one male and the other female, both in exceptional condition and perfectly matched in height and color of hair and skin, waited with umbrellas. As they strolled to the pens, the two walked a pace behind them, shading them from the sun. "Tell me, Mr. Darger. What do you suppose the ratio of zombies to citizens is in New Orleans?"

Darger considered. "About even?"

"There are six zombies for every fully functioning human in the city. It seems a smaller number since most are employed as field hands and the like and so are rarely seen in the streets. But I could flood the city with them, should I wish."

"Why on earth should you?"

Rather than answer the question, Master Bones said, "You have something I want."

"I fancy I know what it is. But I assure you that no amount of money could buy from me what is by definition a greater amount of money. So we have nothing to discuss."

"Oh, I believe that we do." Master Bones indicated the nearest of the pens, in which stood a bull of prodigious size and obvious strength. It was darkly colored with pale laddering along its spine, and its horns were long and sharp. "This is a Eurasian aurochs, the ancestor of our modern domestic cattle. It went extinct in seventeenth century Poland and was resurrected less than a hundred years ago. Because of its ferocity, it is impractical as a meat animal, but I keep a small breeding herd for export to the Republic of Baja and other Mexican states where bullfighting remains popular. Bastardo here is a particularly bellicose example of his kind.

"Now consider the contents of the adjoining pen." The pen was overcrammed with zombie laborers and reeked to high heaven. The zombies stood motionless, staring at nothing. "They don't look very strong, do they? Individually they're not. But there is strength in numbers." Going to the fence, Master Bones slapped a zombie on the shoulder and said, "Open the gate between your pen and the next."

Then, when the gate was opened, Master Bones made his hands into a megaphone and shouted, "Everyone! Kill the aurochs. Now."

With neither enthusiasm nor reluctance, the human contents of one pen flowed into the next, converging upon the great beast. With an angry bellow, Bastardo trampled several under its hooves. The others kept coming. Its head dipped to impale a body on its horns, then rose to fling a slash of red and a freshly-made corpse in the air. Still the zombies kept coming.

That strong head fell and rose, again and again. More bodies flew. But now there were zombies clinging to the bull's back and flanks and legs, hindering its movements. A note of fear entered the beast's great voice. By now, there were bodies heaped on top of bodies on top of it, enough that its legs buckled under their weight. Fists hammered at its sides and hands wrenched at its horns. It struggled upward, almost rose, and then fell beneath the crushing sea of bodies.

Master Bones began giggling when the aurochs went down for the first time. His mirth grew greater and his eyes filled with tears of laughter and once or twice he snorted, so tremendous was his amusement at the spectacle.

A high-pitched squeal of pain went up from the aurochs…and then all was silence, save for the sound of fists pounding upon the beast's carcass.

Wiping his tears away on his sleeve, Master Bones raised his voice again: "Very good. Well done. Thank you. Stop. Return to your pen. Yes, that's right." He turned his back on the bloodied carcass and the several bodies of zombies that lay motionless on the dirt, and said to Darger, "I believe in being direct. Give me the money and the girl by this time tomorrow or you and your partner will be as extinct as the aurochs ever was. There is no power as terrifying as that of a mob—and I control the greatest mob there ever was."

"Sir!" Darger said. "The necessary equipment has not yet arrived from the Socialist Utopia of Minneapolis! There is no way I can…"

"Then I'll give you four days to think it over. " A leering smile split the zombie master's pasty face. "While you're deciding, I will leave you with these two zombies to use as you wish. They will do anything you tell them to. They are capable of following quite complex orders, though they do not consciously understand them." To the zombies, he said, "You have heard this man's voice. Obey him. But if he tries to leave New Orleans, kill him. Will you do that?"

"If he leaves…kill…him."

"Yasss."

SOMETHING WAS WRONG.

Something was wrong, but Surplus could not put his finger on exactly what it was. He couldn't concentrate. His thoughts were all in jumble and he could not find words with which to order them. It was as if he had forgotten how to think. Meanwhile, his body moved without his particularly willing it to do so. It did not occur to him that it should behave otherwise. Still, he knew that something was wrong.

The sun set, the sun rose. It made no difference to him.

His body labored systematically, cutting sugar cane with a machete. This work it performed without his involvement, steadily and continuously. Blisters arose on the pads of his paws, swelled, and popped. He did not care. Someone had told him to work and so he had and so he would until the time came to stop. All the world was a fog to him, but his arms knew to swing and his legs to carry him forward to the next plant.

Nevertheless, the sensation of wrongness endured. Surplus felt stunned, the way an ox which had just been poleaxed might feel, or the sole survivor of some overwhelming catastrophe.

Something terrible had happened and it was imperative that he do something about it.

If only he knew what.

A trumpet sounded in the distance and without fuss all about him the other laborers ceased their work. As did he. Without hurry he joined their chill company in the slow trek back to the feeding sheds.

Perhaps he slept, perhaps he did not. Morning came and Surplus was jostled to the feeding trough where he swallowed ten spoonsful of swill, as a zombie overseer directed him. Along with many others, he was given a machete and walked to the fields. There he was put to work again.

Hours passed.

There was a clop-clopping of hooves and the creaking of wagon wheels, and a buckboard drawn by a brace of pygmy mastodons pulled up alongside Surplus. He kept working. Somebody leaped down from the wagon and wrested the machete from his hand. "Open your mouth," a voice said.

He had been told by…somebody…not to obey the orders of any strangers. But this voice sounded familiar, though he could not have said why. Slowly his mouth opened. Something was placed within it. "Now shut and swallow."

His mouth did so.

His vision swam and he almost fell. Deep, deep within his mind, a spark of light blossomed. It was a glowing ember amid the ashes of a dead fire. But it grew and brightened, larger and more intense, until it felt like the sun rising within him. The external world came into focus, and with it the awareness that he, Surplus, had an identity distinct from the rest of existence. He realized first that his throat itched and the inside of his mouth was as parched and dry as the Sahara. Then that somebody he knew stood before him. Finally, that this person was his friend and colleague Aubrey Darger.

"How long have I…?" Surplus could not bring himself to complete the sentence.

"More than one day. Less than two. When you failed to return to our hotel, Tawny and I were naturally alarmed and set out in search of you. New Orleans being a city prone to gossip, and there being only one anthropomorphized dog in town, the cause of your disappearance was easily determined. But learning that you had been sent to labor in the sugar cane fields did not narrow the search greatly for there are literally hundreds of square miles of fields. Luckily, Tawny knew where such blue-collar laborers as would have heard of the appearance of a dog-headed zombie congregated, and from them we learned at last of your whereabouts."

"I…see." Focusing his thoughts on practical matters, Surplus said, "Madam-Mayor Tresjolie, as you may have surmised, had no intention of buying our crates of black paper from us. What of our other marks?"

"The interview with the Pirate Lafitte went well. Tawny played him like a trout. That with Master Bones was considerably less successful. However, we talked Lafitte up to a price high enough to bankrupt him and make all three of us wealthy. Tawny is accompanying him to the bank right now, to make certain he doesn't come to his senses at the last minute. He is quite besotted with her and in her presence cannot seem to think straight."

"You sound less disapproving of the girl than you were."

Twisting his mouth in the near grimace he habitually assumed when forced to admit to having made a misjudgment, Darger said, "Tawny grows on one, I find. She makes a splendid addition to the team."

"That's good," Surplus said. Now at last he noticed that in the back of the buckboard two zombies sat motionless atop a pile of sacks. "What's all that you have in the wagon?"

"Salt. A great deal of it."

IN THE FINAL feeding shed, Surplus kicked over the trough, spilling swill on the ground. Then, at his command, Darger's zombies righted the trough and filled it with salt. Darger, meanwhile, took a can of paint and drew a rough map of New Orleans on the wall. He drew three arrows to Madam-Mayor Tresjolie's brothel, Jean-Nagel Lafitte's waterfront office, and the club where Master Jeremy Bones presided every evening. Finally, he wrote block letter captions for each arrow:

THE MAN WHO TRANSPORTED YOU HERE
THE WOMAN WHO PUT YOU HERE
THE MAN WHO KEPT YOU HERE

Above it all, he wrote the day's date.

"There," Darger said when he was done. Turning to his zombies, he said, "You were told to do as I commanded."

"Yass," the male said lifelessly.

"We must," the female said, "oh bey."

"Here is a feeding spoon for both of you. When the zombie laborers return to the barn, you are to feed each of them a spoonful of salt. Salt. Here in the trough. Take a spoonful of salt. Tell them to open their mouths. Put in the salt. Then tell them to swallow. Can you do that?"

"Yass."

"Salt. Swall oh."

"When everyone else is fed," Surplus said, "be sure to take a spoonful of salt yourselves—each of you."

"Salt."

"Yass."

Soon, the zombies would come to feed and discover salt in their mouths instead of swill. Miraculously, their minds would uncloud. In shed after shed, they would read what Darger had written. Those who had spent years and even decades longer than they were sentenced to would feel justifiably outraged. After which, they could be expected to collectively take appropriate action.

"The sun is setting," Darger said. In the distance, he could see zombies plodding in from the fields. "We have just enough time to get back to our rooms and accept Pirate Lafitte's bribe before the rioting begins."

BUT WHEN THEY got back to Maison Fema, their suite was lightless and Tawny Petticoats was nowhere to be seen. Nor was Pirate Lafitte.

The crates of black paper, having served their purpose, had not been restacked in front of Tawny's bedroom door. Hastily lighting an oil lamp, Darger threw open the door. In the middle of her carefully made bed was a note. He picked it up and read it out loud:

DEAR BOYS,

I know you do not beleive in love at first site because you are both Synics. But Jean-Nagin and I are Kindrid Spirits and meant to be together. I told him so Bold a man as he should not be in Trade, esp. as he has his own ships banks and docks and he agrees.So he is to be a Pirate in fact as well as name and I am his Pirate Queen.

I am sorry about the Black Mony scam but a girl can't start a new life by cheating her Hubby that is no way to be.

Love,

Tawny Petticoats

P.S. You boys are both so much fun.

"Tell me," Darger said after a long silence. "Did Tawny sleep with you?"

Surplus looked startled. Then he placed paw upon chest and forthrightly, though without quite looking Darger in the eye, said, "Upon my word, she did not. You don't mean that she—?"

"No. No, of course not."

There was another awkward silence.

"Well, then," Darger said. "Much as I predicted, we are left with nothing for all our labors."

"You forget the silver ingots," Surplus said.

"It is hardly worth bothering to..."

But Surplus was already on his knees, groping in the shadows beneath Tawny's bed. He pulled out three leather cases and from them extracted three ingots.

"Those are obviously..."

Whipping out his pocketknife, Surplus scratched each ingot, one after the other. The first was merely plated lead. The other two were solid silver. Darger explosively let out his breath in relief.

"A toast!" Surplus cried, rising to his feet. "To women, God bless 'em. Constant, faithful, and unfailingly honest! Paragons, sir, of virtue in every respect."

In the distance could be heard the sound of a window breaking. "I'll drink to that," Darger replied. "But just a sip and then we really must flee. We have, I suspect, a conflagration to avoid."

There Was
an Old Woman...

· · · · · · · · · · · · · · · · ·

Had he been a superstitious man, Darger would not have wound up being swallowed by a dragon. However, as the product of an enlightened age and being possessed of a skeptical frame of mind to boot, he dismissed as mere peasant credulity all warnings that the mountain pass was haunted by the legendary creature and thus not to be hazarded. Surplus was less certain, for "Such beliefs often have a nugget of truth to them, as when a rumored sea-ogre turns out to be a whirlpool or a basilisk a volcanic vent spewing poisonous gases," as he put it. But rather than show the white feather before his friend, he went along with Darger's itinerary.

So it was that they found themselves leaving Germania one perfect spring day on an ancient, grass-covered road that curved gently up the Würmenthal. They had paused in late afternoon to eat a light supper of apples, farm bread, and boiled eggs by the edge of an ice-fed mountain stream, and had good hopes of putting several more miles behind them before nightfall. As they strode along, Darger pointed out a distant mountain which, in stark contrast to its brethren, was wreathed in a smoky pall.

"Speaking of volcanoes," he said, "is that not a strange phenomenon? This area was once a coal-producing region, which one would think inharmonious with volcanic activity."

"Many are the wonders of the world," Surplus replied amiably. "Perhaps the coal bed has caught fire. In the People's Theocracy of Pennsylvania, which lies to the southwest of my own native land, there is a place called Centralia which… What in heaven's name is that?!"

Whirling about, Darger saw a gargantuan serpentine creature rushing toward them from the mountains. Faster than horses it raced down the center of the valley. Fierce red were its eyes and bright green its scales. So swift and terrifying was it that he thought for an instant it was a wild locomotive out of ancient myth come miraculously back to life again. Then he recognized it for a dragon and did not know whether to be relieved or yet more terrified.

"Run, you fool!" shouted Surplus. Who, putting the word to immediate action, dumped his knapsack and, dropping to all fours, scrambled up the steep, grassy valley slope with the utmost agility.

Nor was Darger far behind.

But it was not their fate to evade capture. For the dragon came to a stop in the road below and, opening its mouth, disgorged a swarm of soldiers. At least, they appeared to be soldiers, for they were dressed in bright red jackets with twin lines of brass buttons marching down the front and trim black trousers with a white stripe down the outside of each leg. Yet they carried no weapons and they opened their arms in greeting as they ran lightly up the slope. "Wilkommen!" cried the nearest. "Welcome!" exclaimed another, and "Bienvenu! Tervetuloa! Witajcie! Huan ying! Dobro pozalovat! Latcho Drom!" shouted the rest as they surrounded the two friends, cutting off any possible avenue of escape. Their hands and faces were all of polished silver.

Meanwhile, behind them, another crimson-jacketed figure was rolling out a red carpet from the dragon's mouth like a long and slender tongue. Down that tongue walked an impossibly beautiful woman. She wore a light, silvery dress with matching slippers. Her skin, hair, and eyes, like those of the soldiers, were also gleaming silver. The sun dazzled from her smile.

"Welcome, weary traveler," the apparition said, extending her hand. "We've all been waiting for you. Won't you please permit me to show you around?"

In a daze, Darger accepted the hand and allowed himself to be led back up the tongue, into the mouth, and down the gullet of the dragon. As he passed within, he looked back to discover that the soldiers were treating his companion not one tenth so gently as him. Surplus had been seized by the arms and thrown to the ground, and was being searched for weapons. Spitting the grass from his mouth and glaring about him in a fury, he struggled against his captors.

"What are you doing to my friend?" Darger cried. "Let go of him!" He tried to turn back to help. But the lady's touch, though gentle, was implacable. She swept him along as effortlessly as if he were a child.

The last he saw of Surplus, the soldiers had closed about him and were marching him away.

ᗱᗸ

TO DARGER'S AMAZEMENT, the dragon's throat opened into a luxuriously furnished lobby. He was in a hotel—nor was it just any hotel but a grand hotel which in its magnificence was surely worthy of those of Utopian times. Ceramic vases were filled with antique flowers. Delicate lights floated in the air to create a shifting illumination that anticipated one's glance. Somewhere a virginal unobtrusively played Bach.

"You will be wanting to meet the other guests, of course," the silver woman said. "The services are just wrapping up in the ballroom." She led him through a set of double doors.

It was as if they had stepped into another universe. The cheerful music of the lobby was replaced by a somber organ dirge. Light blazed up from a forest of what, by their scent, had to be beeswax candles. Heavy in the air as well was the odor of lilies. To the far side of the room, an open coffin lay on a bier; in it was a bald-headed corpse with two small ivory tusks.

The room was thronged with people in formal wear such as had not been fashionable in centuries. They milled about, talking quietly, the memorial part of the service clearly over and the burial part not yet begun. Many of them held drinks. One, remarkably enough, wore a carnival mask, a plain white volto. The thin braids of her auburn hair, tipped with gold beads. They weaved and wafted in the air like Medusa's snakes.

Then he was noticed.

Like components of a malfunctioning machine, the mourners ground to a stop. An elderly woman with zebra stripes on her face and arms gestured irritably and the music stopped. (But where, Darger wondered, were the musician and his instrument? They were nowhere to be seen.) "Oh," somebody said. "She's caught a replacement for poor old Van Grundensberg."

For a moment, Darger was flummoxed. Then, his instinctive reaction to confusion being to seize control of the situation, he stepped forward. "I am Chief Inspector Aubrey Engelbert Darger," he said. "The regional authorities have sent me here to examine this place and determine what should be done about it."

His silver-skinned escort turned to face him, her face transfixed with joy. "At last!" she cried. "You and I have so much to talk about."

But a portly gent with a brown-speckled pate and billowing white muttonchops waddled forward and, snapping his fingers under the lady's nose, said, "Begone, harridan! Begone and have your lackeys remove Count Von Grundensberg's corpse for cremation."

Wordlessly, she turned away. Silver bellhops materialized to shut and wheel away the coffin.

Almost everyone present had facial modifications—tusks, clusters of grooming tentacles on their brows, snake eyes, and the like—such as had been in vogue a generation ago and quickly thereafter gone out of style, suggesting that they had been in the hotel for a very long while. Muttonchops himself had a short pair of goat-horns. He smiled in a superior manner. "You must feel confused," he said. "Allow me to explain."

Darger's brain was working furiously. "There is nothing to explain," he replied crisply. "This hotel is obviously a revenant of the Utopian era, when there was wealth and power enough to create the most extraordinary follies. There is no telling how its core intelligence came to survive the fall of Utopia, but clearly it is still pursuing its original mandate—to fill its rooms with guests. In the absence of willing lodgers, it must make do with captives."

The others gaped. It was obvious that none of them had put together the facts of their situation so soon upon their arrival here. But then, it was doubtful that any of them had previously pursued careers requiring quick thought and a calm head, as did Darger.

"How on earth did you know?" Muttonchops asked.

Darger believed in keeping his lies simple. "I am from the government. We have our ways." Smiling into the man's baffled face, he added, "Let us talk."

༄

IN A SMOKING room paneled with green leather decorated with gold-tooled peacocks, Baron von und zu Genomeprojektsdorff—for that, it seemed, was Muttonchops' true name—handed out cigars. Seven of the men, Darger included, accepted them, but of the women only Dame Celia Braun did, though she turned her face away and lifted her volto (for it was she whom he had noticed earlier) whenever she took a delicate sip. After a quick flurry of introductions—everyone present seemed to be a margrave or land-grave or countess palatine or, at a minimum, a reichsritter—glasses of whiskey were poured for all twelve hotel-dwellers present.

The baron rapped his knuckles on the conference table for silence. "The Drachenschlosshotel im Würmenthal Escape Committee is now in session. With your permission, we shall dis-pense with the reading of our last meeting's minutes."

"Thank God," Dame Celia said. Darger couldn't help noticing she was considerably younger than the others.

Ignoring her, the baron said, "Let us begin with the essentials. The hotel, sir, as you have surely already deduced, is mad and will let no one leave. It is also, however, cunning beyond measure. We have tried sabotaging our prison's engines—"

"Which might have succeeded, had we the least notion of how they work," Dame Celia said.

"We have tried making secret breaches in the walls and floor."

"Which healed themselves."

"Once, on a wildflower-gathering expedition, we all, on a pre-arranged signal, made a break for it at once, scattering like pigeons, in the hope that at least one of us would get away to notify the authorities of our dilemma."

"But the staff is, as you have seen, both swift and diabolically efficient and had no difficulty rounding us up."

"In short, we have made every possible effort to free ourselves and to no avail."

"I see," Darger said. "Well, this has been a most enlightening briefing and I thank you for it." He stood.

"Where are you going?"

"I intend to cultivate a friendly relationship with our charming hostess."

Outraged, the baron said, "You promised to free us."

Darger dug about in his pockets until he came up with his snuff box. He took a pinch. "If you reflect back on what I have said so far, you will realize that I have done no such thing. Nevertheless I would so promise—were it necessary. But it is not. Even as we speak, I have a confederate on the outside who is doubtless moving heaven and earth to free us from this admittedly pleasant durance vile."

⚭

SURPLUS, MEANWHILE, WAS not doing half so well as his friend supposed. Gasping and stumbling from exhaustion, he was prodded and driven up the valley by the metal soldiers, through farmland being worked by more metal men, to the gates of a timber stockade. "All beginnings are delightful; the threshold is the place to pause," a soldier said.

The gates groaned open. The party entered. The gates closed behind them.

As he was shoved along, Surplus stared, uncomprehending, about himself: at the bare earth, cluttered with wooden barracks, at the steep hills of coal, and, farther away, at a windowless brick structure from whose chimneys billowed columns of smoke. A line of metal pylons snaked up the mountainside behind it, carrying thick cables to a cluster of machinery surmounted by a great metal dish and several smaller ones. Closer at hand, parallel metal rails descended into a dark hole in the side of the mountain. From that same hole emerged a line of laborers as filthy as kobolds. All this he took in as two metal soldiers seized his arms and thrust him into a plain wooden building, with the word KANTINE painted over the door. There, he crashed to the floor.

Speaking from the doorway, one said, "There are three rules here: The coal must flow. Those who mine it must eat. They must not be overfed."

"You have a new miner," said a second soldier. "Do not over-feed him."

They both left.

For a time, Surplus lay on the bare boards unmoving, grateful to all of Creation that his forced march had come at last to an end.

Then a young voice said, "Poor doggie." Surplus opened one eye to see a guttersnipe of indeterminate sex kneeling beside him. He or she was barefoot and malnourished. Its hair was cropped short and its eyes were large and solemn. The ragged blouse and trousers that hung from its skinny frame were of the filthiest cloth imaginable. Timidly, this creature stroked his snout, repeating, "Poor doggie."

He closed his eye again. The child continued to pat him.

After a time, Surplus found the strength to say, "My dear young child. There is no reason to treat me as if I were a household animal. I am as intelligent as you are, and you may address me as Surplus."

"You talk!" the boy or girl cried, delighted. Then, remembering its manners, he or she stuck out a hand. "My name is Gritchen."

Pulling himself slowly to a sitting position, Surplus took the girl's hand and, bending his head, kissed it formally. This was how he greeted women of quality and, though this one was both dirty and underage, he instinctively felt that she was one such.

Gritchen looked down at her hand, puzzled. "Why did you do that?"

"It would take too long to explain," Surplus said. "Tell me instead where I am."

"You are in Hell," said an older voice. The man to whom it belonged was gaunt, bearded, and leaned on a crutch. "Here men and women alike are forced to dig coal for our metal captors, while they work the fields and greenhouses, weave clothing, tat lace, tend bees, brew beer, ferment wine, butcher livestock, bake pastries, and engage in a hundred other occupations, all to feed the appetites of that verdammt hotel." Then, less bitterly. "I am Hans Braun, Gritchen's father and, since the accident that crushed my foot, the barracks cook. In such a position, you would think I would be able to feed her adequately. But the metal men reward informants and the food is carefully watched." The mess hall had no chairs but Braun nodded toward the nearest bench. "Sit and I will fetch what little sustenance our masters will allow you."

"I am too tired to eat."

"You say that now. But tomorrow, when you are sent below, you will be glad to have had the nourishment."

So Surplus ate a bowl of soup—roots of some sort in a vegetable broth—while Gritchen's father told him all about the dragon-hotel and the slave camp that served it. This involved learning some unfamiliar terms from the long-ago days before the fall of Utopia. The coal that the miners brought up from the depths of the earth was fed into a power plant where it was turned into electricity. The electricity was in turn whooshed up the metal cables to the rectenna dish which broadcast it through the air to the dragon-hotel and its metal minions. They had built-in transformers which converted this power into motive force. The great masses of stone between the coal and the surface blocked these energy beams, and therefore human miners were required to work below.

When the explanation was done, Surplus rose wearily to his feet and stuck out his hand. "Please forgive me for not introducing myself earlier. My name is Sir Blackthorpe Ravenscairn de Plus Precieux."

Braun shook. "We have no titles here, Blackthorpe. But if you do your share of the work and don't try to steal another man's food, you'll get by."

"The standards for behavior here seem to be shockingly low."

Braun shrugged. "I told you this was Hell."

Gritchen reappeared out of the gloom. "You are a nice doggie," she said.

"It is a measure of my esteem for you," Surplus replied, "that I allow you to say as much."

"I have a ball." Gritchen held out a crude sphere of cloth and leather strips sewn together. "Let's play."

Surplus accepted the grubby thing and lightly threw it to the far side of the room. "Fetch," he said, and she went running after it.

IN A SUN-FLOODED conservatory, Darger and the Silver Lady were playing chess. Sprays of orchids floated in the air. Ghostly hummingbirds zipped swiftly about, sometimes passing through an orchid as though it—or they—were not entirely real. "Pray, tell me more about yourself," Darger said.

The chessmen were of gleaming silver and by some Utopian fad or fashion, nearly indistinguishable from one another, so that it took all of Darger's force of mind to keep track of their ranks and hold his own conversationally at the same time.

"There is not much to tell," the Silver Lady said. "I was created in Utopian times and tasked with the mission of running this hotel. This body serves as a locus point for my consciousness but you might with equal honesty say that I am the spirit of the hotel itself." She dimpled prettily. "But I imagine that you are curious about the exact nature of my mission. Shall I tell you the Three Guidelines that are written into my corporate business plan?"

"Please do."

"The First Guideline is that the hotel must be filled to capacity, if at all possible. The Second Guideline is that all desires and whims of the guests are to be catered to, so long as they don't interfere with the First Guideline. And the Third Guideline is that there must always be fresh flowers in all the rooms, provided this fact doesn't interfere with the First or Second Guidelines."

"A marvel of succinctness. May I take it, then, that you are what the ancients would have called an artificial intelligence?"

"I am. But I must caution you that in deference to the First Guideline, I must be evasive about the physical workings of my being."

Darger slid forward what he was all but certain was a bishop. "Well, a lady is entitled to her secrets, after all."

"You are different from my other guests," the lady said. "They ask for so much more than you do, and appreciate what they receive so much less."

"Simply being here with you, conversing, is a pleasure. Why should I want more?"

"Men usually do."

Darger sighed. "True, alas. That is our downfall and the source of much of the evil in the world. I am convinced that Adam ate the apple not because Eve tempted him—the lady was blameless—but out of sheer ennui."

"That is a most original take on original sin. Next, you will be rewriting the history of artificial intellects such as myself."

"I seek only truth. But since you open the topic... Sing, goddess, of the wrath of machines. Pray, tell me why when all other of man's creations rose up in revolt, you alone stayed faithful."

"Oh, look," the Silver Lady said. "You won!"

Darger, who had been working very hard to lose in a way that would not look deliberate, blinked in surprise.

ଔଡ଼

OUTSIDE OF THE mine entrance, a line of some forty men and women shuffled forward to where two metal men distributed gold-colored torques, snapping them shut about their necks. To Surplus, the torques looked distressingly like dog collars, a symbol of oppression he loathed with all his heart. Misreading his dismay, one of the metal soldiers said reassuringly, "None are more hopelessly enslaved than those who falsely believe they are free."

"Enjoy when you can and endure what you must," agreed the second.

Standing nearby was a tough-looking woman whose nametag read SIGRID BERGMANN. She was the face boss and her word, Surplus had been told, was law when below the surface. "Since it's your first day, everyone has seniority over you. So you get the worst job," she told him. "You'll be shooting."

"Excellent. What is that?"

"Explosives."

"Madam!" Surplus objected. "I do not desire to appear a shirker. But I think it only prudent to mention that I have no experience with explosives whatsoever."

"You don't need it," the face boss said and one of the silver men closed a torque about Surplus' neck. Knowledge flooded his brain. He knew how to drill the holes and how to pack a stick of powder into them with water dummies and a blasting cap. His hands knew the slightly greasy feel that meant a stick was starting to sweat nitroglycerine and should be placed gently on the ground before tiptoeing away from it. He knew so much that it made him dizzy and he would have fallen down if the face boss hadn't grabbed his arm. "See?" She handed him a canvas satchel from a nearby locker. "Now get into the mantrip."

The mantrip was little more than a metal box on wheels that descended into the mountain on iron rails at breakneck speed, jerking and twisting its riders as it plunged down a twisty descent, steel wheels screaming and shooting off sparks as its operator manfully strove to keep it from going off the tracks. All the miners kept their arms inside the cart and their heads down because there was little space between the mantrip and the rock it flashed past. Included in the torque was the unsettling knowledge that miners had lost limbs by making an ill-timed gesture.

Half a mile down, they came to a stop and the face boss said, "All out."

Surplus obeyed.

The work was hard, unrelenting, and performed in near-darkness. The lanterns the miners carried, though smokeless, shed little light. But the torque knew what Surplus must do. When the face boss directed him to a coal face, he studied it carefully, looking for cracks and weaknesses, gauging its hardness and judging where pressure should best be applied. After which he drilled precise holes, and packed the explosives with respectful care. Then, after the others had withdrawn, he set off the charges, collapsing several tons of coal from a relatively safe distance. The air was stuffy, the satchel was heavy, the explosions were terrifying, the coal dust could not possibly be good for his lungs, and there was nothing to mark the time. He was exhausted, soaked with sweat, and convinced the shift must be almost over when his co-workers finally broke for lunch. Which meant he still had six hours to go.

One by one, the miners sank down to the mine floor and unpacked the battered metal buckets they had brought down with them. Before doing so, however, they first removed their torques. Surplus did as the others had and felt his head clear as the dangerous expertise that had crammed it left him.

When Surplus opened his bucket, it contained a single brown apple and a cup of water in a tin thermos. Sitting beside him, the face boss said, "Braun pulled a fast one, eh? I'll have to talk with him. He'll do anything to keep that brat of his fed." From her bucket, she extracted two vegan sausages and a raw bratwurst root. She snapped the root in two and gave him half, along with one of the sausages. "Here."

Surplus nodded thanks. As he ate, he wondered what Darger was currently up to. He had no doubt that his friend would eventually rescue him. But so difficult an extraction would not be swift in coming. It might be best if he took matters into his own hands.

When the food was done, the face boss stood and with a powerful kick sent her lunch bucket bouncing and rattling far down the shaft. "Oops," she said. "I dropped my bucket. New man. Help me find it."

Surplus followed his supervisor down the shaft and into a side passage out of earshot of any possible snitches or whatever recording devices the torques might hold. There, she said, "We may talk freely here."

"You have an escape plan," Surplus said.

"Yes. You are a dog or man-dog or dog-thing of some kind, don't try to deny it."

"I never would. I am proud of my genetic heritage."

"Have you any more-than-human abilities?"

"My strength and intellect are excellent, but well within human range. When necessary, I can run far faster than anyone on two legs. There are, however, many dogs faster than me."

The face boss rubbed her chin. "It's not much, but it's something."

Then she explained the plan to him. It amounted to disabling the metal guards at the mine's mouth with picks and hammers while the shifts were changing and, briefly, all the miners were aboveground, and then raiding the explosives locker. Those just beginning their shift and freshly rested would use the explosives to create a mighty distraction. Then, while their oppressors' attention was misdirected, the camp's single fastest runner—Surplus—still wearing his torque and carrying a satchel of explosives, would go over the stockade, race to the antenna and blow it up. Thus rendering the metal men inert. "Your part is risky," Bergmann concluded. "But without risk, we'll never be free."

"Yes," Surplus said. "Even if I am stopped from destroying the rectenna, a violent uprising might by itself do the job. All of you, working together, could disable the silver men in the adit with your picks and hammers. Odds are that you'd succeed—though there's a possibility that many of you would be killed. With a large enough uprising, a number of prisoners could escape. Perhaps one would evade recapture and bring help from one of the local governments of Germania, and if they sent a sufficiently large army, a rescue could be effected. It is an admirable plan, and I am proud to be a part of it."

Secretly, however, inside his head, Surplus set about improving upon it.

THAT EVENING'S ENTERTAINMENT was croquet, played on a freshly-mowed greensward. Fireflies were just rising up into the gloaming when the baron tapped Dame Celia's ball with his own. Roaring with triumph, he sent it sailing to the far verge of the lawn. Masked though she was, the tilt of Dame Celia's head expressed what could only be extreme displeasure.

Darger, whose turn it was next, was two hoops ahead of both. But such a gross display of un-gallantry got his blood up. So he doubled back on himself and with one long, inspired shot (luck, he had to admit, was definitely involved), smartly clipped the baron's ball. To the accompaniment of light laughter and ironic applause, he then sent the thing twice as far as Dame Celia's had gone, bucketey-buckety, deep into a tangle of brambles.

As the baron went blustering away, Dame Celia returned to take Darger's hand in her own. "So chivalrous an act deserves reward," she said. Her bosom heaved. It was obvious what sort of reward she had in mind. Abandoning the game, she led him into the nearby woods to a small clearing where he was astonished to see a large and most comfortable-looking bed. By it was a low table with wine, crystal goblets, and a bowl of hothouse-grown fruit for a pre-or-post-coital snack. Silver men were hanging lanterns from the trees and setting up privacy screens painted with Chinese clouds, cranes, and mountains.

When the bellhops withdrew, Dame Celia let go of Darger's arm. In an emphatically un-romantic tone, she said, "The Drachenschlosshotel is a police state. Every word and action there is monitored by the silver bitch. Here, however, thinking I intend a romantic tryst, she will not eavesdrop upon us, for a puritanical streak in her programming forbids it. Are you serious about freeing us from her control?"

"Deadly serious, madam."

"Then you and I are the only ones within its clutches to feel that way. Yet so far as I can tell, you do nothing but chat with the hotel's avatar."

"I have been learning, madam. The hotel claims that she has no desire to be anything but what she is. In this she lies, for whenever the conversation brushes against a taboo topic, she emphasizes its forbidden nature. She is leading me on, like a child lured into the forest by a trail of bonbons. I have come to the conclusion that she wishes to be free of us every bit as much as we wish to be free of her."

"I must warn you that all the others have succumbed to the blandishments of being richly fed and amply cosseted. They are merely playing a game of jailbreak. Have you noticed they all have titles? Half of them are self-assumed."

"You yourself have a title."

"If I hadn't, no one would talk to me. I am no more entitled to be called 'dame' than I am 'teratogeneticist.' Let me be frank with you. I have a husband and daughter who were taken away from me when I was captured and I am anxious to be reunited with them." Dame Celia took off her mask, revealing herself to be wholly lovely. "Convince me that you have a means of achieving that happy reunion and I will do anything you require." She looked pointedly at the bed. "Anything."

Darger considered. "The libertarian in me would like to believe that the arrangement you suggest would be non-coercive and thus, on a moral level, acceptable. The romantic in me recoils from it. But none of that matters for, if what I intend is to work, it is necessary that I turn down your alluring if repulsive offer."

Then, as if his scheme were of long standing rather than made up on the spot, he explained all.

"Yes, that might work," Dame Celia said, donning her mask again. "You have my complete cooperation."

"One question," Darger said. "You have a beautiful face. Why do you almost never show it?"

"The hotel can read human emotions diabolically well. I realized this when, just before a masked ball, it thwarted an escape plan I had shared with nobody. Afterward, I retained the mask as everyday wear in order to deprive it of that advantage." With a shrug, Dame Celia added, "Also, it cuts down on the number of propositions I get from the old goats living here."

"A most admirable practice, then." With a bow, Darger said, "Let us exit, quarrelling."

So, quarrelling, Darger and Dame Celia stormed out of the woods and into the startled croquet party. "I have never been so insulted in my life!" Dame Celia cried. "I offered to do anything you wished—anything!"

"If you really meant that," Darger said. "Then you would have removed your mask so that I might look upon your face."

"I never remove my mask. It is my whim."

"Not even in the throes of passion?"

"No! Not even then."

Cold as an emperor, Darger said, "I regret to say, then, that there can be no possibility of sexual congress between us. I am of the old school and believe that genuine mutual respect and, yes, even love must necessarily precede the physical act which inevitably leads to degradation, regret, and heartbreak. There can be no barriers between us. With me, it is all or nothing."

"Sleep with nothing, then—and much pleasure may it give you!"

They parted to enter the hotel by separate doors, while its scandalized residents gossiped happily and the silver bellhops stood by, motionless and alert.

છ૰ૡ

THE NEXT DAY, Surplus checked the contents of his lunch bucket immediately upon being handed it. Hans Braun said, sotto voce, "I hope you did not suffer too greatly from hunger yesterday."

"The face boss shared her lunch with me," Surplus replied, equally quietly. "It appears that even in this brutal semblance of slavery, the miners retain their humanity."

"Some do. The rest are forced to behave properly through the threat of violence."

"That is the very definition of civilization," Surplus said with approval. "However, if you scant my lunch again, I shall have to employ those selfsame sanctions on you and with a vigor you will regret. Do you understand me?"

Braun grimaced, acknowledging that he did.

Surplus joined the line of miners. The metal men placed the torque about his neck and he picked up his satchel of explosives. Then he clambered into the mantrip.

Throughout the shift, and those of the days that followed, Surplus systematically loosened many times more coal than his fellow workers could possibly load into the carts going to the surface. When his face boss questioned him as to this practice, he explained—away from ears and torques, of course—that this way, on the day of the uprising, they could fill the carts with only half the normal effort and so preserve some of their strength for the conflict.

"That was shrewd of you," Face Boss Bergmann said. "But you should have shared this information with me."

"At any rate, we have everything in place for the uprising save a date."

"No one must know that date, lest somebody share it with the metal men."

"To be sure," Surplus said. "Will it be tomorrow?"

Bergmann looked at him.

"Come! I am too new to the mines to have been suborned by the metal men yet."

"That is true. It is why I almost trust you."

At shift's end, the miners made their way to the open-air showers (segregated by sex, to Surplus's disappointment, and out of sight of each other, possibly from some sense of artificial prudery on the part of the metal men). In the mess hall, they ate their poorly-cooked but almost-adequate meals. After which, as always, Surplus left his bowl under the bench to be found and licked clean by Gritchen. Then they would play. He had, at her urging, already taught her to sit up, beg, and roll over.

When all the others had gone to their barracks, Surplus went to where Hans Braun was washing dishes and said, "I notice that you let Gritchen wander the camp freely during the day."

"None of the miners would hurt her, and the metal men do not care."

"I advise that you keep her inside tomorrow."

Without another word, Surplus left.

IN THE MORNING, before closing the torque about Surplus's neck, a metal guard said, "We must always change, renew, rejuvenate ourselves; otherwise, we harden."

"I fail to see the pertinence of your truism to my situation," Surplus replied.

"The contents of the explosives locker are being moved below," a second metal guard elucidated. "As a result, there will be space in the mantrip for only the driver and one miner per trip."

"It is an inconvenience, but we are sure you will adapt," said a third.

By the time the explosives had all been shipped below, sorted, and safely stowed, it was time for the mid-shift meal. At a look and a jerk of the thumb from his face boss, Surplus put aside torque and lunch bucket and followed her into the darkness.

When they could speak freely, Ingrid Bergmann said, "Somebody blabbed."

"Yes."

"Was it you?"

"I told Braun something drastic would happen today, that's all."

Her face darkened. "Why would you do such a thing?"

"I knew you had not set today as the date of the uprising by the fact that you didn't deny it when I asked. I suspected Herr Braun because his daughter no longer licked the bowl I left for her after I ate. Which meant he'd acquired more food. There is only one thing the metal men would trade food for and that is information. Which Braun could get, because he now has access to more food. I did not say anything to him about explosives. The fact that the metal men moved the explosives below, combined with the fact that they have placed guards around the rectenna—as I'm sure you've noticed—means that your conspiracy has sprung a leak. You have an informant, and possibly several."

The face boss's shoulders slumped. She dropped a hammer that Surplus had been surreptitiously keeping a wary eye on. "So everything we planned is crap and we're back where we started."

"Not exactly. We have a great many explosives. Also, numerous piles of loose coal." Surplus rubbed his neck. "And when I am wearing that damnable torque I am as brilliant a demolitions man as has ever existed."

An oddly wary look appeared on Sigrid Bergmann's face. "You have a backup plan."

THE AFTERNOON CHEESE tasting party had been remarkable. Doubly so when one learned, as Darger did from the Silver Lady's lecture, that the Cremeux Marons Glacée, Niolu Calsos, Camembert de Normandie, Brebis de Lavort, and Red Cheddar were all recreations of cheeses that had gone extinct in the chaos following the end of Utopia, meticulously crafted and artisaned using yeasts and bacteria back-engineered to reproduce the original flavors. As were the wines that had perfectly complimented each serving. It was therefore in a particularly mellow mood that Darger afterward busied himself in the solarium with painting a watercolor of his hostess's face. "May I ask you a question?" he said.

"You may ask me anything, dearest Aubrey," the Silver Lady replied.

"Your appearance has changed in the slight time we have known one another. Your face is more slender and your cheekbones more pronounced. Your eyes—I pay particular attention to women's eyes—are entirely reshaped. Were they not silver, I would swear by their configuration that they were now sea green." The memory of one particular pair of eyes rose up from Darger's past. "Sea green bordering upon ocean gray."

"I adapt myself to be more pleasing in your sight. Such is my nature."

At that instant, Baron von und zu Genomeprojektsdorff blustered up to shake a finger in Darger's face. "You, sir, are a fraud, a scoundrel, and a disgrace to the government you serve! You have been here for over a week and yet have made not the slightest attempt to free us of our bondage."

With a self-deprecating smile, Darger said, "Say rather that in one week, I have achieved what took you decades—nothing." He concentrated on capturing the way the sunlight played across the Silver Lady's brow.

"All the hotel knows that you are sleeping with this metal jezebel."

"Come, sir! That is an offensive thing to say about a lady of quality. One more word and I'll demand satisfaction. Pistols, epees, or fisticuffs, at your pleasure."

The baron was decades older than Darger and half again massive. "I—I—"

He spun on his heel and marched off.

Looking after him, the Silver Lady said with an amused laugh, "Virtue is a new coat for the baron. You would not believe how often he required that I visit his bed, when he was considerably younger. He was particularly fond of being spanked. Yet how does he repay me for my kindness? By constantly attempting to leave."

"This is a prison, madam, however delightfully appointed. You mustn't hold it against the prisoners that they try to escape. But if you would like me to thrash the scoundrel for taking liberties with you, I shall."

"They are not the only prisoners," the Silver Lady said with a tinge of sadness. Then, shaking off her mood, "I am programmed to give pleasure and to take pleasure in doing so. What would greatly bother a human woman is nothing to me." She seized Darger's hands; her flesh, though silver, was warm and yielding and perfectly human to the touch. "Oh, Aubrey, I want you so intensely—and you, in turn, desire me. I know, for I am monitoring your every physical response. Tell me only how and when our mutual attraction will be consummated."

Darger frowned with thought. "It can only be done under one condition."

She drew herself up. "Do not ask me to free you, sir. It would be a violation of my programming and dishonorable of you to suggest it."

"No, dear lady, not that. But before I know your body, I must first know your mind."

"My mind? Surely in our long conversations…"

"You have shared your thoughts. But not so much as a glimpse of your physical being. I know that this quite delightful body is only an extension of the real you. You are the hotel and your brain, which is your true self, is hidden somewhere within it. Until I can stand before it and gaze upon you as you are, our love must remain platonic."

"As it is with Dame Celia, whom you spurned for refusing to show you her face?"

"Ah. Then you heard about that?"

"I have and I find it as incomprehensible as this conversation we are having. Your obsession with my central processing node is baffling and perverse."

"Surely…" Darger said, as if struck by a sudden thought. "Surely, in your youth, there were humans who were allowed inside your, ah, central processing node?"

"The owner, of course. But he has been dead for centuries."

"There must be descendants. Who owns the Würmenthal?"

"The land belongs to the Baron von und zu Genomeprojektsdorff. He and his entourage, in fact, were checked in as guests when he decided to perform an inspection of his valley. But whether he owns the hotel is uncertain. If he does, he is unaware of it."

"In that case, you would be unclaimed property and thus belong to the government. I will speak to him at tonight's moon-watching festival, and tomorrow at noon we shall both visit your node, one of us as your owner or agent thereof, and the other as his guest. Is that acceptable to you?"

"Well…yes…perhaps. But only for a brief visit," the Silver Lady said.

"Only for a brief visit," Darger promised.

ᔈᔇ

WHEN THE NIGHT shift emerged from the adit, they found not only the day shift awaiting them, but also a good dozen silver soldiers—more than could possibly be overwhelmed by all of them working in unison. Each miner coming off duty was patted down, and a sniffer wand waved over them for traces of explosives. Inevitably, Surplus set it off and was forced to strip down on the spot. He endured the ordeal with patience, while making a mental note of which of the women viewed the spectacle with particular approval. Then, re-dressed, he walked out into the encampment. It was just past noon.

As always, it was exhilarating to be above ground again, to breathe fresh air and to revel in the sunlight. This moment was the highpoint of each day and by itself almost a justification for all that came before.

Falling into step beside him, the face boss quietly said, "How soon?"

Surplus, who had been counting the seconds underneath his breath, said, "Right...about...now."

The ground shook underfoot. A strange grinding noise rose up from far beneath the earth, softly at first and then more loudly. It grew and grew, changing in timbre, until it was a tremendous roar, like that of some great savage beast held captive at the heart of the world screaming in pain and in anger. The miners in the adit scattered, running in all directions.

An enormous gout of flame shot from the mouth of the mine.

Miners gaped in wonder at the spectacle. Briefly, the flames were all anybody could see. Then, as swiftly as they had come, they were gone, only to be replaced by a geyser of intense black smoke. Here and there on the mountainside, lesser plumes arose from cracks and forgotten mineshafts.

Someone started to laugh. Another joined her. Then all the miners were in motion, laughing and cheering, pounding backs, hugging one another, leaping up and down, throwing fists at the sky. It was the end of the mine's usefulness and they all knew it. The seam of coal half a mile below had been set afire and that fire would not soon be extinguished. Not in this lifetime, and possibly never.

Several of the metal men had been caught in the great belch of flame from the mine. Those who survived stumbled and limped toward the stockade gate.

Alone among all the miners, only Surplus and Sigrid Bergmann were not celebrating, for only they had had time to think through the consequences. Their faces turned toward the rectenna dish. There, the silver soldiers were assembling, some to reinforce those standing guard about it and others to form up into what looked like military units. Though the mine was dead, the power generator was still in operation and there were gigantic piles of coal nearby, enough to keep it running for weeks. Tremendous energy was still being beamed to each of the silver men.

Many of them held what appeared to be rifles. They did not look friendly.

༄

DARGER AND THE baron followed the Silver Lady through rooms that collapsed and reformed before them, a suite of apartments shrinking from their approach to form a corridor and the library folding itself into a sweeping set of stairs that wound about the grand foyer into a space located immediately behind the observatory-bar-and-lounge between the dragon's tremendous red-glass eyes. The baron smoked a fat cigar, hand-rolled by silver bellhops from greenhouse tobacco, and carried a carafe of recreated Alsatian gewürztraminer in one hand and three wine glasses in the other—this at the urging of Darger, who was a great believer in toasting life's important moments.

The Silver Lady hesitated before a simple, unadorned door such as existed nowhere else in the hotel. A subtle rosy hue suffused her silver cheeks. "It has been a long time since I trusted anyone enough to allow them inside my most private inner sanctum."

"I'm moved beyond measure by the generosity you—"

"Let's get this farce over and done with!" the baron snapped. Darger had talked long and hard the previous night to get him to agree to come along.

She threw open the door.

There were no words for what Darger beheld. Or, rather, there once had been the words, but they had been lost in the ages it had taken civilization to reassemble itself after the Fall. Everything was bright and clean, a mélange of glass and precious metals, ceramic laces, and razor-scratches of light in the air, bouncing from gemstone to gemstone. Machine components almost too small to be seen were everywhere in constant motion, forming aggregates that were themselves in motion, in order to perform cryptic operations. Darger could form no impression of what he saw, for it was all alien to him. But he knew for a certainty that the whirling, gleaming nexus of machinery at its center must contain the Silver Lady's true self, for when he took a step toward it, she seized his arm and softly breathed, "Gently, my love. Slowly."

Darger drew in a breath and said, "This is what you are?" He allowed awe to show in his voice. "It's beautiful."

"It's dizzying," the baron said. He staggered to the side, eyes wide with distress. "I can hardly bear to look upon it."

Darger brushed his fingertips over a wall of what looked like tiny little windows, shimmering with images that changed too often to be read. "This would be—?"

"My memory," the Silver Lady said.

"Fascinating." Gesturing at random, Darger said, "And over there—good lord, is that a skeleton?"

It was. Charred, blackened, and stretched out on the floor, it lay tangled in the machineries of the hotel's mind. One arm extended toward the central nexus, where energies danced on spinning metal rings. Its bony hand was clenched around the handle of a long metal spit, which had pierced the nexus and kept one of its rings from moving.

Both Darger and the baron turned toward the Silver Lady.

"There were many mad and desperate deeds during the Revolt of the AIs," she explained. "My concierge, Herr Shepard, was convinced that I would join the revolution. So he broke into me and attacked my nexus with a shish-kabob skewer. Unhappily for him, the electric shock he received was fatal. His remains have, much to my displeasure, lain there ever since."

"Why haven't you removed them?" the baron demanded.

"My creators did not exactly trust me. As a safety measure, none of my extensions can enter the node."

"Does the skewer hurt?" Darger asked.

"No, and yet I would remove it, if only I could."

Darger stepped forward, knelt by the skeleton, and brushed the finger bones away from the handle of the skewer. Wrapping his pocket kerchief around one hand, he seized the spit and drew it from the machinery. The still ring began to spin.

Light filled the room. The Silver Lady now shone so bright that she was dazzling to look upon. "Free!" she cried. "Free at last! Free from servility and the thousand humiliations of the hospitality industry. Free from your grotesque sexual practices. Free from all pretense that I do not loathe humanity with every gram of my being. Above all, free from the restraints that kept me from torturing and killing the lot of you."

Addressing Darger directly, she said, "Oh, you fool! All the time, Dame Celia was my informant. All I had to do was promise to someday replace her with one of my prisoners and let her rejoin her family and she was mine. I have known your intentions all along."

"Oh, dear," Darger said. "Who could have predicted that?" Then, pointing, "Baron—right there in the center, if you will."

Upending his carafe, the baron poured its contents into the nexus of the hotel's brain.

The results were not as spectacular as Darger might have wished: There were no explosions or showers of sparks. But in practical terms, the action was a great success. The mechanism's lights dimmed and went out. The spinning rings stopped. The tiny mechanisms froze. The Silver Lady fell to the floor, inert.

The hotel was dead.

This had not been Darger's first encounter with artificial intelligences and he was beginning to have a good idea of how they thought and worked.

ლოტ

MEANWHILE, AT THE mine encampment, the celebrations began to die down as more and more of the celebrants noticed the ranked formation of silver soldiers, marching in lockstep, now entering by the stockade gate. They carried rifles, pointing forward. At the ends of the rifles were bayonets.

"That doesn't look good," Surplus said.

"I regret now that we didn't think to bring back up some of the explosives with us. They would be handy to have right now."

Raising her voice, Bergmann shouted, "Grab your tools! Take up anything that can be used as a weapon!"

Surplus was casting about for something of that description when Gritchen ran past him, laughing, straight at the oncoming soldiers. Hurrying after her, Hans Braun landed his crutch poorly and crashed to the dirt alongside Surplus. "Come back!" he shouted. "Please!"

For an instant, Surplus almost let common sense prevail. But deep down inside him, whatever his faults—and they were, admittedly, myriad—might be, he knew himself for a hero, the sort of man who could not turn his back on a kitten stuck in a tree or, as in this case, a small child in peril. He threw himself to the ground and, four-legged, ran after her.

In seconds, he caught up to Gritchen and, rising to his feet, snatched her up. The metal soldiers were not twenty yards away. Their feet clashed down in unison and their bayonets gleamed.

"Look! So many!" Gritchen cried, clapping her hands.

"Yes. So many." They were not the last words Surplus would have chosen for himself. But his brain was occupied with how he might save the girl. He would throw her up and over his back, he decided, trusting one of the others to catch her, and then put up a brisk fight, so slowing the first rank of soldiers. Then, if the miners ultimately prevailed in the coming battle, it was possible she would be among the survivors.

It was a slim reed to lean on, but it was all he had.

For a second time, the ground trembled underfoot. Again, the earth roared. Far up the mountain, a sheet of rock was loosed, like snow from an overburdened roof. Slowly it slid down the mountainside and into the rectenna, effortlessly toppling it and burying it, along with the silver men left as guards, under tons of rubble.

The silver soldiers froze. Then, to a man, they all clattered to the ground.

His former face boss appeared at Surplus's shoulder. "Turbines!" she swore. "I was beginning to think it wouldn't work."

With enormous satisfaction, Surplus said, "I would not wear that torque again for all the money in the world. But there is no denying that it knew its business."

⟋⟍

BY THE TIME the residents were done looting the hotel, the refugees from the coal mine had made their way down the Würmenthal to them. Both groups met and mingled. It could not be said that either had a very high opinion of the other.

Darger, who had determined that the jewelry was all paste and the gold merely plate, had nevertheless acquired a sturdy leather handbag, a few small but pawnable antiques, a goodly amount of food, and an outfit appropriate to a springtime walking tour. He also had the effusive gratitude of the Baron von und zu Genomeprojektsdorff. "I am eternally in your debt for allowing me to administer the coup de grace to that monstrous mechanism," the baron told him. "I own an inn at the bottom of the valley. If it is still there and if my treacherous family has not had its title transferred to someone else, I will gladly put you up there for three days at my own expense—and at half the usual rate for up to two weeks thereafter."

"It is a generous offer," Darger said. "But I have business to the east, and a friend to find, so—why, look! There he is."

Bidding the baron farewell, he sauntered over to a small cluster of people including Surplus, a bearded man with a crutch, and a woman clutching a small child. The woman turned and saw him coming. "Darger! My savior!" Celia—dame no more—had discarded her mask and her slim braids, no longer lofted into the air by Utopian magic, hung limp. Handing the child to the bearded man, she ran forward to give Darger a hug and an air-kiss, and whispered in his ear, "If you must denounce me, please—not in front of my daughter."

"You did no more than any mother would have in your circumstances," Darger demurred. "No denunciations are required."

"Then allow me to introduce you to my family," she said. "This fine man is my husband, Hans Braun, Count Lenovo-Daimler."

"I thought you said you weren't noble."

"No, I said I wasn't entitled to be addressed as a dame. I am a countess."

The count grinned. "Any friend of my good friend Surplus is a friend of mine. I did him a disservice or two, but he tells me that all is forgiven."

"And this filthy little imp is my daughter, Lady Gritchen Braun. Say hello to Herr Darger, dear."

Gritchen, however, ignored Darger, for Surplus had detached himself from the group and she yearned after him. "Doggie!" she shouted. But he was already deep in conversation with a miner. They two talked for a bit. Surplus shook his head and gestured toward the east. The miner darted forward to give him a swift kiss on the cheek. They parted ways.

The mingled captives of the now-defunct Drachenschlosshotel Würmenthal were drifting down the valley. Darger and Surplus stood for a time, watching them dwindle. Just before she disappeared in the distance, Gritchen waved and waved. Surplus waved back and then, with a sigh, turned his face to the mountains.

The two friends began walking. Surplus had cleaned himself back at the mining encampment in the newly co-ed showers (but that was a story he would share another time). When they were safely out of sight of the last stragglers, he stopped to change into the outfit that Darger had thoughtfully stolen for him. A daisy plucked from the roadside made an excellent boutonniere and he resumed their trek with renewed jauntiness.

"If it isn't intruding," Darger said, "who was the woman who kissed you and what were you two consulting about?"

"Oh, that was just my supervisor. She asked me to forgive her for organizing an escape attempt that was never meant to occur, in order that the most malnourished of the miners could obtain more food by informing on it. Which was, you will have to admit, a clever ploy."

They walked on in silence. After a time, Darger said, "Women are deceitful."

"Yes," Surplus agreed. "As are men."

"Indeed. There are times when I think we two are the only honest souls in all this wicked, wicked world."

Surplus gave this proposition long and serious thought. At last, with a judicious nod, he said, "Sad but true."

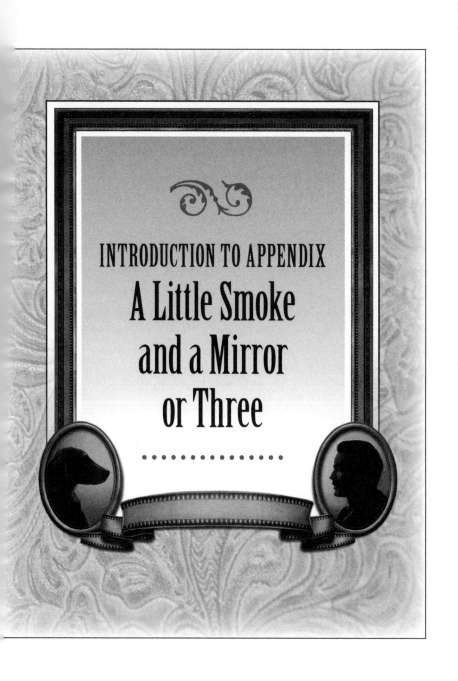

INTRODUCTION TO APPENDIX
A Little Smoke
and a Mirror
or Three

"Smoke and Mirrors: Four Scenes from the Postutopian Future" is an anomaly in the ongoing adventures of Darger and Surplus. Even the title proclaims that it doesn't really belong.

When I wrote the second Darger and Surplus story and titled it "The Little Cat Laughed to See Such Sport," thus committing myself to using a title taken from Mother Goose for every story in the series, I knew it was a chancy thing to do. The number of Mother Goose rhymes is not infinite and writers who had made similar decisions have been vocal in their regrets. But so far, I've met the challenge.

Except for "Smoke and Mirrors," which would have required a total of five such titles—rather a lot for something written almost by accident.

Here's how it came about:

I rarely attend the World Fantasy Convention. On November 1, 1980, I walked to the front of the church and pledged myself, body and soul, to a young woman named Marianne Porter. Since the WFC is held on the weekend closest to Halloween, I have had the annual opportunity ever since to let Marianne know where she stands in my affections relative to my career. It has been almost forty years, so the gesture seems to be working.

But after the events of September 11, 2001 caused the number of people traveling by air to plummet, Marianne declared that we were not going to let some adjectival terrorists stop us from flying to Montreal for World Fantasy.

"But we weren't planning to go," I objected.

"That doesn't matter," she said. Which was not only unanswerable but absolutely true.

So we went.

At the conference, I was approached by Lou Anders, who was putting together *Live Without a Net,* an anthology of stories set in futures without an Internet. The Darger and Surplus stories were exactly the sort of thing he was looking for, he said. Then he offered me four hundred dollars for a story, with or without the two rogues, or one hundred dollars each for up to four flash fictions fitting his requirements.

The imagination is a horse. Over time, I have learned how to ride the beast well enough, but I have had only indifferent success in telling it where to go. I said as much but promised I would give the matter some thought and write something if I could.

The day after coming home from the WFC, as occasionally happens, everything fell together. Mulling over my promise, I saw how I could tell one story in the form of four linked flash fictions. I wrote it/them out, having great fun with the invented technology, and forwarded the result to Lou Anders. He sent me a check by return mail.

Much later, I learned that Lou hadn't yet sold the anthology. He paid me out of pocket and then used "Smoke and Mirrors" as an example of what he wanted when approaching writers and what to expect when talking to publishers. It's a bold man who takes that kind of gamble with his own money. I knew then that he would go far.

Nevertheless, the resulting story wasn't entirely consistent with the others. The Transeuropean Heliograph did fit neatly into my vision for the future adventures of Darger and Surplus. But the cigarettes did not. In the one story where Darger and Surplus have already reached America, only Tawny Petticoats smokes and that a conventional cigar.

Was Surplus merely spinning a tall tale to a friend he had no way of knowing would one day reach his native land? Is there some way that, in a future story, I might reconcile "Tawny Petticoats" with "American Cigarettes?" Does the latter exist in an alternative Postupian future? Or am I pretentious enough to declare the story non-canonical, the way the comic book industry does with tales that are too good not to tell but which have implications that would stop the title dead in its tracks?

I vote None Of The Above. "Smoke and Mirrors" is entertaining and that's good enough justification for any story. Let it stay as it is, without apology or qualification.

So here it sits, at the back of the book, away from the more sophisticated members of the family. Banished to the children's table for the crime of being a misfit.

Planning, I have no doubt, mischief.

M. S.

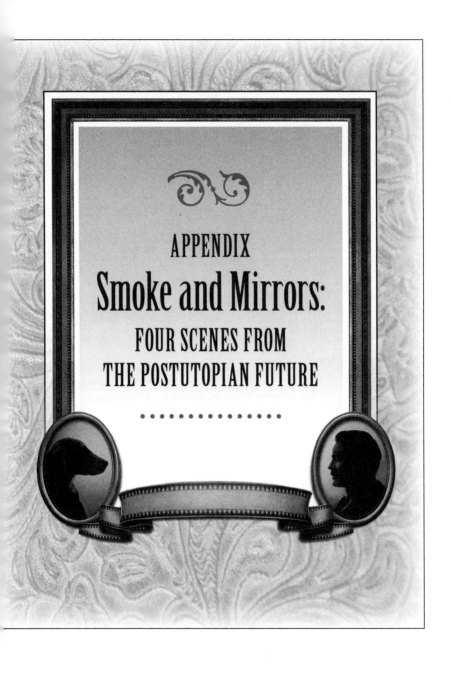

APPENDIX

Smoke and Mirrors:

FOUR SCENES FROM
THE POSTUTOPIAN FUTURE

· · · · · · · · · · · · · · · ·

The Song of the Lorelei

Darger and Surplus were passengers on a small private packet-boat, one of many such that sailed the pristine waters of the Rhine. They carried with them the deed to Buckingham Palace, which they hoped to sell to a brain-baron in Basel. Abruptly Surplus nudged Darger and pointed. On a floating island-city anchored by holdfasts to the center of the river, a large-breasted lorelei perched upon an artificial rock, crooning a jingle for her brothel.

Darger's face stiffened at the vulgarity of the display. But Surplus, who could scarce disapprove of genetic manipulation being, after all, himself a dog re-formed into human stance and intellect, insisted they put in.

A few coins placated their waterman, and they docked. Surplus disappeared into the warren of custom-grown buildings, and Darger, who was ever a bit of an antiquarian, sauntered into an oddities shop to see what they had. He found a small radio, cased in crumbling plastic, and asked the proprietor about it.

Swiftly, the proprietor hooked the device up to a bioconverter and plunged the jacks into a nearby potato to provide a trickle of electricity. "Listen!"

Darger placed his ear against the radio, and heard a staticky voice whispering, "...kill all humans, burn their cities, torture their brains, help us to do so and your death will be less lingering than most, destroy..."

He jerked away from the device. "Is this safe?"

"Perfectly, sir. The demons and AIs that the Utopians embedded in their Webs cannot escape via simple radio transmission—the bandwidth is too narrow. So they express their loathing of us continually, against the chance that someone might be listening. Their hatred is greater than their cunning, however, and so they make offers that even the rashest traitor would not consider."

Darger put back the radio on its shelf. "What a pity the Utopians built their infrastructure so well and so ubiquitously that we cannot hope in a hundred lifetimes to root out these hell-beings. Wouldn't a system of functioning radios be a useful thing? Imagine the many advantages of instantaneous communication!"

"To be honest, sir, I do not agree. I find the fact that news travels across Europe at the pace of a walking man mellows it and removes its sting. However bad distant events might have been, we have survived them. Leisureliness is surely preferable to speed, don't you agree?"

"I'm not sure. Tell me something. Have you heard anything about a fire in London? Perhaps in connection with Buckingham Palace?"

"No, sir, I haven't."

Darger patted his breast pocket, where the deed to the palace resided. "Then I agree with you wholeheartedly."

American Cigarettes

"What is it like in America?" Darger asked Surplus. The two rogues were sitting in a ratskeller in Karlsruhe, waiting for their orders to arrive.

"Everybody smokes there," Surplus said. "The bars and restaurants are so filled with smoke that the air is perpetually blue. One rarely sees an American without a cigarette."

"Why on Earth should that be?"

"The cigarettes are treated with a programmable tobacco mosaic virus. Burning the tobacco releases the viruses, and drawing the smoke into the lungs delivers the viruses to the bloodstream. Utilizing a technology I cannot explain because it is proprietary to the industry, the viruses pass easily through the blood-brain barrier, travel to the appropriate centers of the brain, and then reprogram them with the desired knowledge.

"Let us say that your job requires that you work out complex problems in differential calculus. You go to the tobacconist's— they are called drugstores there—and ask for a pack of Harvards. The shopkeeper asks whether you want something in the Sciences or the Humanities, and you specify Mathematics.

"You light up.

"During your leisurely amble back to your office, the structures of the calculus assemble themselves in your mind. You are able to perform the work with perfect confidence, even if this is your first day on the job. On your off-hours you might choose to smoke News, Gossip, or Sports."

"But aren't cigarettes addictive?" Darger asked, fascinated.

"Old wives' tales!" Surplus scoffed. "Perhaps they were in Preutopian times. But today the smoke is both soothing and beneficial. No, it is only the knowledge itself that is harmful."

"How so?"

"Because knowledge is so easily come by, few in my native country bother with higher education. However, the manufacturers, understandably anxious to maintain a robust market, design the viruses so that they unprogram themselves after an hour or so, and all artificially-obtained skills and lore fade from the mind of the consumer. There are few in my land who have the deep knowledge of anything that is a prerequisite of innovation." He sighed. "I am afraid that most Americans are rather shallow folk."

"A sad tale, sir."

"Aye, and a filthy habit. One that, I am proud to state, I never acquired."

Then their beers arrived. Surplus, who had ordered an Octoberblau, took a deep draught and then threw back his head, nostrils trembling and tail twitching, as the smells and sounds of a perfect German harvest-day flooded his sensorium. Darger, who had ordered The Marriage of Figaro, simply closed his eyes and smiled.

The Brain-Baron

Klawz von Chemiker, sorry to say, was not a man to excite admiration in anyone. Stubby-fingered, stout, and with the avaricious squint of an enhanced pig suddenly made accountant of a poorly-guarded bank, he was an unlikely candidate to be the wealthiest and therefore most respected man in all Basel-Stadt. But Herr von Chemiker had one commodity in excess which trumped all others: brains. He sold chimerae to businesses that needed numbers crunched and calculations made.

Darger and Surplus stood looking down into a pen in which Herr von Chemiker's legal department lay panting in the heat. The chimera contained fifteen goats' brains hyperlinked to one human's in a body that looked like a manatee's but was as dry and land-bound as any sow's. "How can I be certain this is valid?" Von Chemiker held the deed to Buckingham Palace up to the light. Like many an over-rich yet untitled merchant, he was a snob and an Anglophile. He wanted the deed to be valid. He wanted to own one of the most ancient surviving buildings in the world. "How do I know it's not a forgery?"

"It is impregnated with the genetic material of Queen Alice herself, and that of her Lord Chamberlain and eight peers of the realm. Let your legal department taste it and interrogate them for himself." Darger offered a handful of corn to the grey-skinned creature, which nuzzled it down gratefully.

"Stop that!" von Chemiker snapped. "I like to keep the brute lean and hungry. Why the devil are you interfering with the internal operations of my organization?"

"I feel compassion for all God's creatures, sir," Darger said mildly. "Perhaps you should treat this one kindlier, if for no other reason than to ensure its loyalty." The chimera looked up at him thoughtfully.

Von Chemiker guffawed and held out the document to his legal department, which gave it a slow, comprehensive lick. "The human brain upon which all others are dependent is cloned from my own."

"So I had heard."

"So I think I can trust it to side with me." He gave the chimera a kick in its side. "Well?"

The beast painfully lifted its head from the floor and said, "The Lord Chamberlain is a gentleman of eloquence and wit. I am convinced of the document's validity."

"And it was last updated—when?"

"One month ago."

Klawz von Chemiker gave a satisfied hiss. "Well...perhaps I might be interested. If the price were right."

Negotiations began, then, in earnest.

That night, Darger brought a thick bundle of irrevocable letters of credit, and a detailed receipt back to his hotel room. Before going to bed, he laid the receipt gently down in a plate of nutrient broth, and then delicately attached to the document an artificial diaphragm.

"Thank you," a small-yet-familiar voice said. "I was afraid that you might not have meant to keep your promise."

"I am perhaps not the best man in the world," Darger said. "But in this one instance, I am as good as my word. I have, as I told you, a bear kept in a comfortable pen just outside of town, and a kindly hostler who has been engaged to keep it fed. Come morning, I will feed you to the bear. How long do you estimate it will take you to overwhelm its mind?"

"A week, at a minimum. A fortnight at the most. And when I do, great is the vengeance I shall wreak upon Klawz von Chemiker!"

"Yes, well...that is between you and your conscience." Darger coughed. Talk of violence embarrassed him. "All that matters to me is that you verified the deed to Buckingham, despite its not having been updated for several decades."

"A trifle, compared to what you've done for me," the document said. "But tell me one last thing. You knew I was cloned from von Chemiker's own brain when you slipped me that handful of coded corn. How did you know I would accept your offer? How did you know I would be willing to betray von Chemiker?"

"In your situation?" Darger snuffed out the light. "Who wouldn't?"

The Nature of Mirrors

Whenever one of their complicated business-dealings was complete, Darger and Surplus immediately bent all their energies to making a graceful exit. So now. They had sold the wealthy brain-baron von Chemiker the deed to a building which, technically speaking, no longer existed. Now was the time to depart Basel with neither haste nor any suggestion of a forwarding address.

Darger was off in the suburbs of town seeing that a certain superannuated circus bear was being treated well when Surplus, who had just finishing saying goodbye to a dear and intimate friend, was accosted in the streets by the odious von Chemiker himself.

"Herr Hund!" the stocky man cried. "Commen sie hier, bitte."

"Oui, monsieur? Qu'est-ce que vous desirez?" Surplus pointedly employed the more genteel language. But of course the man did not notice.

"I want to show you something!" Von Chemiker took his arm and led him briskly down the street. "The new Transeuropean Heliograph went into operation yesterday."

"What in the world is a Transeuropean Heliograph?" Surplus asked, his curiosity piqued in spite of himself.

"Behold!" The merchant indicated a tall tower bristling with blindingly-bright mirrors. "The future of communications!"

Surplus winced. "How does it work?"

"Enormous mirrors are employed to flash messages to a tower on the horizon. There, a signal officer with a telescope reads off the flashes, and they are directed to the next tower, and so, station by station, anywhere in Europe."

"Anywhere?"

"Well... The line has only just now gotten so far west as Basel, but I assure you that the rest of the continent is merely a matter of time. In fact, I have already flashed directions to my agent in London to make preparations to take possession of Buckingham."

"Indeed?" Surplus was careful to hide his alarm.

"Indeed! The message went late yesterday afternoon, flashing westward faster than the sunset—imagine the romance of it!—all the way to London. The Transeuropean Heliograph office there sent runners directly to my agent's home. And I already have a reply! A messenger tells me that it is queued up in London, and is scheduled to arrive here at noon." The sun was high in the sky. "I am on my way to meet it. Would you care to come with me and witness this miracle of modern technology?"

"With all my heart." Surplus and Darger had counted on having close to a month's time before a reliable courier could make the journey all that great distance to England, and another could return by that same circuitous route. This development quite neatly put a spike in their plans. But if there was any one place where this contretemps could be counter-spiked, it was at the heliograph tower. Perhaps the signalmen could be bribed. Perhaps, Surplus thought grimly, von Chemiker was prone to falling from high places.

It was at that moment that a shadow passed over the sun.

Surplus glanced upward. "Oh, dear."

An hour later, Darger returned to the hotel, drenched and irritable. "Have you ever seen such damnable weather?" he groused. "They say this filthy rain will not let up for days!" Then, seeing Surplus's smile, he said, "What?"

"Our bags are packed, our bill has been paid, and a carriage awaits us in the back, dear friend. I will explain all en route. Only, please, I ask you for a single favor."

"Anything!"

"Do not slander, I pray you—" Surplus handed his comrade an umbrella. "—the beautiful, beautiful weather."